'I may find another husband.'

'Is this an oblique way of telling me you already have?' he said harshly.

'No. If I had I wouldn't——'

'Wouldn't have let me kiss you senseless last night! Isn't that what happened?'

'No,' she said hotly. 'I was too taken by surprise to resist, that's all. It didn't mean anything other than that.'

'My mistake. I thought it meant a hell of a lot more than that.'

Dear Reader

There's something different about Mills & Boon romances! From now on, in the front pages of all our stories, you'll find a short extract to tempt you to read on, a biography about the author and a letter from the editor, all of which we hope will welcome you to our heart-warming world of romance. What's more, if you've got any comments or suggestions to make about Mills & Boon's stories, drop us a line; we'll be glad to hear from you.

See you next month!

The Editor

Catherine George was born in Wales, and early developed a passion for reading which eventually fuelled her compulsion to write. Marriage to an engineer led to nine years in Brazil, but on his later travels the education of her son and daughter kept her in the UK. And instead of constant reading to pass her lonely evenings she began to write the first of her romantic novels. When not writing and reading she loves to cook, listen to opera, browse in antiques shops and walk the Labrador.

Recent titles by the same author:

LEADER OF THE PACK
OUT OF THE STORM

THE PERFECT SOLUTION

BY

CATHERINE GEORGE

MILLS & BOON LIMITED
ETON HOUSE   18-24 PARADISE ROAD
RICHMOND   SURREY   TW9 1SR

First published in Great Britain 1992
by Mills & Boon Limited

© Catherine George 1992

Australian copyright 1992
Philippine copyright 1992
This edition 1992

ISBN 0 263 77533 X

Set in Times Roman 11 on 12 pt.
01-9205-49600 C

Made and printed in Great Britain

CHAPTER ONE

BY THREE in the afternoon the ordeal seemed endless. But at long last the subdued buffet lunch was over and the mourners began to depart. Reiterating condolences to the pale young widow, some shook her hand, others kissed her cold cheek, closer friends gave swift, sympathetic hugs. Eventually Joanna Clifford closed the door on the final compassionate face, the shell of her composure at cracking point now it was all over.

Except that it wasn't over, quite. There was still some unfinished business to attend to before she came to grips with the everyday reality of widowhood. First on her list of priorities came a vote of heartfelt thanks to Doris Mills. Doris, who normally came in twice a week from the village to help with the housework, had been a tower of strength since early morning, her eagle eye everywhere as the hired caterers served the funeral feast. She brushed aside Joanna's thanks in her usual nononsense manner.

'No trouble at all, Mrs Clifford. I've seen the caterers off and everything's in order. I'll be off now. See you in the morning. There's a nice fresh pot of coffee waiting for you in the drawing-room.'

This last unlooked-for solicitude was almost too much for Joanna. She blinked hard, squeezing Doris's hand by way of thanks, then went back to the drawing-room, where Jim Fowler, financial adviser to her dead husband, waited in front of the fireplace. Joanna poured coffee for them both, then sat back in silence, waiting for him to begin. Jim Fowler was a thin man in his late forties. Through thick-lensed spectacles his eyes peered at her, red-rimmed, their normal shrewd gleam replaced by a blend of grief and misgiving as he confronted his friend's weary young widow. He'd been hit hard, Joanna knew. Jim Fowler and Paul Clifford had been born and brought up in the same part of London's East End, thick as thieves all their lives, each one the only man the other ever trusted.

'How do you feel, Jo?' he asked. 'Really feel, I mean. You look terrible.'

'So do you.' Joanna leaned back in the corner of the sofa, allowing herself to relax now only Jim was there to see. Her eyes met his with a trace of defiance. 'If you want the truth, the only emotion I seem capable of is guilt.'

'*Guilt?* What the devil have you got to be guilty about? It's Paul——' He stopped, biting his lip.

'I feel guilty, Jim,' went on Joanna, eyeing him curiously, 'because after five years of marriage surely I should feel some grief for Paul! But at the moment I don't. There's a great deal I need explained before I can bury my dead. So start talking, Jim.'

He gazed at her hopelessly. 'I feel like one of those old-time messengers who got their heads chopped off when they brought bad news.'

Joanna smiled sadly. 'Don't worry, Jim. I'm handier with a garden trowel than a hatchet.' She looked towards the window, her eyes heavy. 'In fact I was planting wallflowers when the police arrived to tell me Paul was killed. They were so kind. They even made tea for me in my own kitchen. For shock.' She turned her head to look Jim in the eye. 'More shock than they knew. I thought Paul was in America. Instead he was smashing himself up in his Ferrari right here in the UK. And he wasn't alone in the car when he did it, either.'

Jim rotated his head wearily to ease his tense neck muscles. He sighed. 'All right, love. I wish it weren't me who had to tell you. But I will.'

Joanna sat up, bracing herself, her eyes like blue flames in her pale face. 'Thank you, Jim. Perhaps afterwards I can get on with the rest of my life.'

He nodded, opening the briefcase he was never without. He looked across at her with a wry smile. 'In those old films it was always the family lawyer who got this job, not a run-of-the-mill accountant.'

Joanna, who knew that Jim Fowler was a great deal more than that, paid close attention as the shrewd financial adviser took over from the family friend. Jim began by explaining that Paul's factories had taken a recent hammering due to high interest rates and fierce competition.

'To put it in a nutshell, PC Plastics is in a bad way, Jo.'

'How bad?'

'On the verge of bankruptcy——'

'*Bankruptcy!*'

'Paul's trip to the States was a last bid to save it from the chop.' He rubbed a hand over his face wearily. 'It was no use. He came back early. Even if he'd lived it would still be curtains for PCP.'

Joanna stared at him in shock. 'Dear heaven, Jim, I had no idea. Paul never said——' She stopped short, shrugging. 'But then, Paul rarely said anything at all to me lately.' She frowned in concern. 'But what will happen to you, Jim—and all the others?'

He shrugged. 'Don't worry about me. I've got plenty of irons in the fire. And the rest are young enough to find jobs. You need to look out for yourself, love.'

There was a brief, tense silence. Joanna's mouth took on a bitter curve as she looked about her at the familiar, comfortable room. 'Rather a joke if I'm forced to sell the house in the end, after all.'

Jim mopped his forehead with a handkerchief. 'It needn't come to that. This house is your personal property. The mews cottage in Chelsea will have to go, of course.'

'But Paul sold that years ago!'

'No, he didn't. He—well, he just told you he did.'

Her eyes widened. 'What are you saying?'

Jim looked miserable. 'I wish there was some way I could put this that wouldn't sound like a slap in the face. But there isn't.'

'Oh, for crying out loud!' snapped Joanna, suddenly at the end of her tether. 'Get on with it, Jim.'

'He kept the Chelsea place because——' Jim swallowed. 'Because that's where he spent a lot of his time when he wasn't down here with you.'

She stared at him blankly. 'What are you talking about? He always stayed at his club.'

'Did you ever speak to him there?'

She thought for a moment. 'No—now I come to think of it, I suppose not. I left messages when necessary, which was once in a blue moon.'

Jim nodded. 'He stayed there part of the week, the rest of the time he went off to Chelsea—and Rosa.'

Joanna felt the colour leave her face. Jim sprang to his feet, but she waved him away, managing a smile. 'I'm all right.' She leaned forward to pour herself more coffee, her hand shaking only slightly as she filled the cup. She sipped in silence, then raised blank blue eyes to Jim Fowler. 'Who is Rosa? No need to ask, I suppose. There was bound to be another woman. For years all I've been to Paul is a presentable doll to produce for special occasions.'

'Not in the beginning.'

'No,' she repeated in a dead voice. 'Not in the beginning.' There was an awkward silence. 'This Rosa,' went on Joanna after a while. 'I suppose she was the passenger with him in the crash?'

Jim nodded.

'And did she survive?'

'Only for a few hours.' Jim came to sit beside her, taking her cold hand in his. 'Jo, I'd give anything in the world to avoid hurting you like this——'

'But you knew,' she said dully. 'You knew all the time.'

'Yes, love. So did my Maisie. But we couldn't tell you.'

'No. I can see that.' Joanna shrugged. 'Right. So Paul had a mistress. I don't know why I'm making such a fuss. Besides, as Marlowe says, "the wench is dead". And so is Paul.' Suddenly her self-control disintegrated. Snatching her hand away from Jim, she turned her face into the sofa cushion and gave way to the tears she'd kept at bay for days.

Jim watched in anguish for a moment, then bent over her, patting her shoulder awkwardly. It was a long time before Joanna could pull herself together. She accepted the starched handkerchief he offered, mopping herself up vigorously.

'Sorry,' she croaked when she could speak.

'Nothing to be sorry for, girl. You needed to let go.'

'I suppose so.' Joanna sat straight. 'But don't misunderstand. I'm crying for myself, Jim. Don't pretend you don't know what it was like between Paul and me lately. Because of his religion there was no possibility of divorce. But he wouldn't hear of a separation. To him it was a public admission of failure, and Paul hated failure.' Joanna looked up sharply. 'Jim—he didn't—I mean the accident wasn't some kind of suicide attempt, was it, because Paul failed to get American backing?'

Jim looked shocked. 'Not with Rosa in the car, Jo!' He shifted in his seat uncomfortably. 'Besides, Paul was brought up a strict Catholic, remember. He'd never have killed himself.'

'But he did, in the end, didn't he?' Joanna sighed heavily. 'It's getting late. You should be getting back to Maisie. How's her arthritis, Jim?'

'Bad. That's why she isn't here today. She wanted to come. I wouldn't let her.'

'Give her my love. Tell her I'll come and see her.'

'She told me to bring you back with me tonight, wants you to stay with us for a bit.'

Joanna shook her head. 'Tell your lovely wife I'm grateful, but for the moment I'm better on my own—heaven knows I'm used to it.'

Jim reached across for his papers. 'If that's what you want, Jo. If you change your mind, any time, you know where to come. Now. Sorry to keep at you, but I'd like to get the financial position straight before I go.'

'I won't touch a penny of Paul's money,' said Joanna vehemently.

'Now then, love. I can understand how you feel. You've had a bloody awful shock.' Jim smiled tiredly. 'But you'll feel different tomorrow. You love this house. And if you refuse any money at all you might have to sell it.'

'Perhaps I should! If it weren't for this place things might have been a lot different. On the other hand,' she added bleakly, 'you know where you are with a house.'

Jim gave her an unhappy look, then plunged into a morass of facts and figures. The factory itself, although no longer viable as a going concern in its present form, was situated on land wanted urgently by a property developer. Once the sale had gone through the widow of Paul Clifford could not only keep her home, but live there in reasonable comfort.

'So if I could just have Paul's will, Joanna,' said Jim, standing up.

She frowned. 'Haven't you got it?'

'No. It wasn't with the rest of the papers. I assumed it must be down here.'

'Paul never mentioned it. Perhaps it's in his desk in the study. You look for it, Jim. I'll make more coffee.'

But when Jim rejoined her in the drawing-room he looked grim. 'Not a sign of it. I suppose it could be in the Chelsea house.'

Joanna shrugged. 'Perhaps he altered it in favour of his mysterious Rosa. Cut me off with the proverbial shilling.'

'Don't talk like that! Have a look upstairs, please,' said Jim rather sharply. 'The damn thing must be somewhere.'

Paul Clifford had been obsessive about tidiness. The search through his belongings, though undertaken with reluctance, took Joanna no time at all.

'Sorry,' she said, as she rejoined Jim. 'Nothing. Not even a scented billet-doux in one of his pockets. Paul covered his tracks very efficiently—the same way he did everything else.'

'Try not to be bitter, Jo. Paul was proud of you in his own way. Rosa was—was something separate.'

Joanna bit back a cutting retort. 'Was she, indeed! Just who the blazes was she, anyway? Rosa what?'

'Rosa Anstey. She was Paul's secretary for years. You used to know her quite well.'

Joanna's eyes widened incredulously. 'Miss Anstey! Are you serious?' She shook her head, trying to take it in. 'But I was very fond of Paul's invaluable Miss Anstey. She was such a friendly person, warm dark eyes and rather plump—not even very young!' She stared at him blankly. 'I assumed Paul's mistress would be some brainless young bimbo.'

Jim took in a deep breath. 'Jo. There's something else——' He broke off as the telephone interrupted them.

Joanna answered it then handed it over to Jim in consternation. 'Jim, it's for you. Maisie's had a fall!'

Jim barked a few staccato sentences into the receiver, then crashed it back on the handset, looking distraught. 'She's in hospital. Tried to reach something on a high shelf and fell. Broken her leg.' Feverishly he stuffed papers in his briefcase, then raced outside to his car, with Joanna hard on his heels. He opened the car window, and waved a peremptory finger at her. 'Look for that will again, Jo.'

'Stuff the wretched will!' snapped Joanna. 'Just get yourself off to Maisie, and you mind you ring me tonight and tell me how she is!'

Joanna watched the car out of sight then went back into the house, utterly shattered by Jim's various revelations. Then, as she looked about her at the square familiar hall, she became conscious, for the first time in years, of feeling totally alone. The house felt eerily empty. She shook off the feeling impatiently. She was used to solitude here. Paul had never been in the house for more than two or three days at a time during their entire marriage. Their holidays together, such as they were, had been spent abroad.

And the rest of his life had belonged to Rosa Anstey.

I wonder, thought Joanna bitterly, what Rosa did on weekends? Did she have a weekend lover, in the way that I had a weekend husband? What did I lack that plain, unassuming Rosa Anstey was able to supply?

She paced through the familiar rooms of her home like a tigress in a cage, humiliation and resentment burning inside her. If Paul's mistress had been younger and sexier than herself it would have been easier to bear. But Rosa Anstey had been ten years older and so thoroughly *nice*.

Joanna made a sudden dash for the stairs, wrenching down the zip of her dress as she went, unable to bear her mourning black a moment longer. She ran into her bedroom, peeling off the dress as she went. She pulled on a bright yellow sweatshirt and faded Levis, thrusting her feet into ancient old sneakers, the type of clothes Paul had detested. She tugged the pins from her hair, releasing the heavy, straight weight of it to brush it until it shone like expensive butterscotch against the creamy pallor of her face. Red patches of colour burned along her cheekbones as she wielded the brush, accentuating the kingfisher-blue of eyes which gazed back at her in defiance. Portrait of Joanna Clifford, widow, she thought scathingly.

She turned away, her attention caught by the king-sized bed. It was hard to believe now that Paul had ever shared it with her. Now he never would again. In the beginning it had been so different. In the early days of their marriage he would rush her upstairs to bed the minute he arrived for the weekend, eloquent in his delight with the bride who made him feel like a young stud again. But all that had ended, abruptly, long before their first anniversary. Nothing was ever the same again. She sighed. What a gullible fool she'd been never to suspect that Paul had a mistress.

The struggle to come to terms with her husband's long-term infidelity bleached the transient colour from Joanna's face. She slumped down on the bed in deep depression, huddling there for a long, black interval, until the telephone shrilled, intruding on her misery. Who, she thought in despair, could possibly want to talk to her tonight, of all nights? Only the possibility that it might be Jim Fowler moved her to pick up the receiver at last.

'Mrs Clifford?' asked an unfamiliar male voice. 'Yes.'

There was a pause. 'My name is Marc Anstey——'

Joanna dropped the telephone. She grabbed at it, her hand shaking as she put the receiver to her ear.

'Hello?' said the caller. 'Mrs Clifford? Are you still there?'

'Yes,' she said tonelessly. 'I'm still here. Would you repeat your name, please?'

'Anstey. Marc Anstey. And it's very important that I see you as soon as possible. Tonight, if you will.'

'No!' she said vehemently. 'I mean—this isn't a good time. There's been a funeral here today.'

'I know.' The voice was distinctive, with a gravel-based timbre which hinted of origins other than Anglo-Saxon. 'I've just been to one myself, Mrs Clifford—Rosa's funeral. She was my sister.'

Joanna was silenced. 'I'm sorry,' she said after a moment. 'But why should you want to see me, Mr Anstey?'

'I promised to deliver something to you. From Rosa.'

Joanna felt suddenly cold. 'From Rosa? I don't understand.'

'It's not something one can discuss over the phone,' he said curtly. 'If you'd be kind enough to spare me a few minutes I'd be grateful, Mrs Clifford. I won't keep you long. I quite understand your reluctance to talk to me under the circumstances, but I promised Rosa I'd get in touch with you personally to carry out her wishes.'

What about my wishes? thought Joanna with resentment. 'Oh, very well, Mr Anstey. Where are you?'

'About a mile away in the village. I can be with you in ten minutes.'

'Make it half an hour, please,' she said firmly.

'Very well. Half an hour, then. And thank you,' he added.

Joanna replaced the phone in a daze, wondering if her nervous system could stand much more in the way of shocks. What could Rosa's brother want with her?

She wondered whether to change back into the black dress, but decided against it. This Anstey man could take her as she was. In her particular circumstance mourning black was sheer hypocrisy anyway.

By the time the doorbell rang Joanna had herself firmly under control, all her defences shored up and ready as she opened the door to face a man who was enough like Rosa Anstey to confirm his identity. But where Rosa had been round and plump this man was tall and lean, a curious look on his face as he took in her appearance.

'Mr Anstey, I presume,' she said coolly. 'I'm Joanna Clifford.'

He nodded, taking something from a pocket to hold out to her. 'Would you like some identification?'

Surprised, Joanna took the yellow card from him. The photograph and signature confirmed not only that he was Marc Anstey, as he said, but also that he was a member of the National Union of Journalists, and worked for the *Sentinel*, one of the major national newspapers.

Her eyes flew to his face. 'You're a journalist?' She almost threw the card back at him. 'If you're here in a professional capacity, Mr Anstey——'

'Of course I'm not,' he said wearily. 'I'm on leave. And I don't deal in gossip, Mrs Clifford. I'm a foreign correspondent for the *Sentinel*. My business with you here tonight is strictly personal.'

Joanna looked at him in silence for a moment, then held the door open. 'I suppose you'd better come in.'

'Thank you.' Her unwelcome visitor stood very still in the hall, watching her as she bolted the door. He looked like she felt, thought Joanna. His close-curling black hair gave a spurious impression of youthfulness contradicted by his olive-skinned face, which was haggard with grief. His black eyes narrowed a little as he registered her appearance.

'I've just changed,' Joanna said without thinking, then could have bitten her tongue. What she chose to wear was nothing to do with her unwelcome visitor.

'Did your heart sing a gay *Te Deum* as you discarded your widow's weeds?' he asked, his voice accentless, but with a gravelly huskiness even more pronounced now they were talking face to face.

Joanna stared in affront. 'I beg your pardon!'

He rubbed a hand over his face wearily. 'I apologise. To you and to Noel Coward. The last thing I want is to antagonise you, Mrs Clifford.'

She opened the drawing-room door and motioned him through. 'Perhaps you'd better sit down and tell me what it is, precisely, that you do want. And what it can possibly have to do with me.'

Marc Anstey took the chair she indicated, looking bleak and self-contained, and nothing at all like Joanna's idea of a journalist in a dark, well-cut suit, his black tie reminding her all too forcibly of his connection with Rosa Anstey, aka Paul Clifford's mistress.

'I'm sorry to intrude at what must be the worst possible time for you.' He looked at her levelly. 'At the moment I'm based in Washington, but as luck would have it I'd just arrived on leave in the UK when the accident happened. I managed to get to the hospital in time to be with Rosa before she died.' His jaw tightened as he reached a hand into an inside pocket and drew out a long, legal-looking envelope. 'Before she died Rosa gave me this and told me to bring it to you.'

Joanna took the envelope from him, trembling inside at the thought of what it might contain.

'Would you read it, please?' he said tersely. 'I can't stay long. I've got someone with me in the car.'

Joanna sat down on the edge of the sofa, her face set. 'It must be very important, Mr Anstey, to bring you here the very day of my husband's funeral.'

His mouth took on a sardonic twist. 'It was not an errand I relished, believe me.'

Joanna drew a document from the envelope, unsurprised to find she was looking at the last will and testament of Paul Clifford, dated only weeks before his death. It was brief enough to read very rapidly. To his wife, Joanna Clifford, he bequeathed the painting by Stubbs from the Chelsea house. To James Frederick Fowler, lifelong and devoted friend, he left his gold watch and cufflinks. To Rosa Maria Anstey he bequeathed the company known as PC Plastics, or whatever sum was received for the sale of said company, this sum to be used for the education of Paola Anstey. In the event of Rosa Anstey's death the legacy would pass to said Paola Anstey, daughter of Rosa Anstey and Paul Clifford.

Joanna read through the document a second time in disbelief. Paola, she thought in anguish, daughter of Paul Clifford. Marc Anstey, watching her closely, leaned forward abruptly.

'Are you all right?'

Joanna nodded, ashen-faced. Marc Anstey gave a quick glance round the room, then went over to the silver salver on a side-table, poured brandy into a glass and brought it back to her. 'Drink some of that. You'll feel better.'

'I loathe brandy,' she protested.

'It'll do you good.'

Joanna took a reluctant sip of Paul's best cognac, vaguely resentful when her visitor was proved right.

'You've had a hard day,' said Marc Anstey stiffly.

'It gets worse as it goes on.'

'Mine hasn't been too wonderful either.' He rubbed a hand over his face.

'No,' agreed Joanna, surprised by an unexpected pang of remorse. 'I imagine not. You were obviously very close to your sister.'

He nodded grimly. 'I loved Rosa very much. Otherwise, Mrs Clifford, I wouldn't be here right now. Rosa begged me to come, made me promise as she—as she was dying. I've always dismissed deathbed promises as so much melodramatic poppycock. When they happen to one personally it's a different kettle of fish, believe me.'

Joanna nodded. 'I know.'

He frowned. 'But I thought your husband was killed instantly.'

'He was. My particular promise was made to my father.'

'Were you able to keep it?'

'At some personal cost, yes.' Joanna regarded the haggard, attractive man with curiosity. 'Is your promise anything to do with me, then, Mr Anstey?'

'Yes, very much so.' He looked her in the eye. 'There's no point in beating about the bush, Mrs Clifford. I've come here to make a suggestion you're going to find totally unacceptable. Insane, in fact. By way of explanation, you have to understand that my sister couldn't bear to think of her child in the hands of strangers. She knew that owing to the nature of my work I can't care for my niece myself for the time being. So Rosa made me swear I'd come to see you in person and ask *you* to take Paola, your husband's child, until I'm in a position to do so myself.'

Joanna stared at him incredulously, her face so pale again he moved towards her swiftly, but she held up her hand. 'I'm not ill—just appalled that you should use such emotional blackmail. Whatever vow you made to your sister is nothing to do with me, Mr Anstey. It's—it's outrageous. You can't possibly expect me to do such a thing!'

He lifted one shoulder in a gesture which contrived to convey derision, hostility and scorn all at once. 'I don't. I never thought for a moment you'd agree. It was my sister, not I, who was convinced you were the right one to have her child.'

'I can't think why!'

He looked her over assessingly. 'Having met you, neither can I, Mrs Clifford.' He met her outraged eyes levelly. 'But there's something you've overlooked. By the terms of Paul Clifford's will Paola now owns PC Plastics. However, Rosa left a will, appointing me trustee to look after my niece's interests. And if I block the sale of PCP to the developer all its present resources will be swallowed up to meet its debts, including your house, Mrs Clifford.'

CHAPTER TWO

JOANNA stared at him, her blue eyes icy with outrage. 'May I ask you a question?' she said after a taut silence.

'By all means.'

'If, Mr Anstey, *you* are the trustee in the case, why did your sister want me to take care of the child?'

He shrugged. 'Make no mistake, Mrs Clifford, I couldn't love my niece more if she were my own child. But I'm single, and I lead a peripatetic sort of existence. After spells in Moscow and Tokyo I'm presently based in Washington.' His mouth tightened. 'When Rosa moved into your husband's Chelsea house I took over her studio flat as a London base, but neither the flat nor my lifestyle is suitable for looking after a child.'

'In the circumstances your sister must have been very fond of you to consider you a suitable guardian for her daughter!'

'She was. As I was of her. Rosa knew perfectly well I wasn't in an ideal position to bring up Paola myself—not yet, anyway. But I swore to her I'd see that her daughter received the best of care—and love.'

Joanna nodded, eyeing him. 'I see. So let me just get this straight. I am to have the responsibility of bringing up the child, but you are the—er—treasurer, shall we say?'

22

The black eyes narrowed to a hard gleam. 'Precisely. Not that *I* gain anything, Mrs Clifford. Whatever comes to the child will be held in trust for her. If you had agreed to give her a home an ample allowance would have been yours for your trouble.' He shrugged indifferently. 'I knew it was a mistake to come here. I apologise for my intrusion—believe me, it was the last thing I felt like tonight. Nevertheless, I've now carried out my sister's wishes as I promised, so my part in all this is over. Goodnight.'

'Wait,' said Joanna, springing to her feet. 'What are you going to do?'

He turned, one eyebrow raised. 'Do? About the sale?'

'No, I don't care a damn about the sale!' she snapped. 'I meant what about—about the child?'

He rubbed a hand along his shadowed chin wearily. 'I don't know yet. But I'll think of something. My problem is the time factor. I've only got a week's leave to sort things out.'

Joanna bit her lip, eyeing him. 'Where is—is your niece now?'

'Outside in the car.'

'*What?*'

He shrugged. 'Since Rosa died she tends to cling to me like grim death. A friend of mine came to the funeral with us, and stayed in the car with her until it was over.'

'Is your friend outside in the car too?'

His face hardened. 'No. An hour spent with a crying child put paid to the lady's maternal instincts. The moment the funeral was over she took off in a taxi. I came here alone. Paola was so worn out I just wrapped her up in a rug on the back seat of the car and she went off to sleep—which reminds me, I'd better see if she's all right.'

'Could I see her?' said Joanna impulsively.

'Why?' His eyes narrowed in suspicion.

She looked at him in appeal. 'Look, until tonight I didn't even know she existed. I just want to see her for a moment, that's all.'

Marc Anstey shrugged, then made for the door. 'As you like.'

Joanna followed him outside towards the car parked at the far edge of the gravel circle in front of the house. He put a finger to his lips as he leaned forward to peer into the back seat.

'She's still fast asleep,' he said under his breath. 'I won't open the door. Satisfy your curiosity, Mrs Clifford, then I'll be off.'

Joanna's throat tightened as she gazed through the car window at a tangle of black curls and sleeping, tear-stained face.

'Well?' he demanded in an undertone. 'Have you seen enough?'

Joanna shook her head slowly. 'As she's asleep will you come back into the house for a moment? You can leave the door open to watch out for her.'

'If I must.'

They went back into the hall and stood in the open doorway, both of them looking fixedly at the car rather than at each other.

'Mr Anstey,' began Joanna, choosing her words with care, 'this has all come as a great shock. It's only a couple of hours since I learned about my husband's association with your sister. To discover there's a child as well is hard to take in. I can't think straight. But I'm not heartless. I see your difficulty, and——' she breathed in shakily '—I feel for the child. Deeply. On the other hand you can't expect me to decide something so important as this off the top of my head.'

'I don't *expect* anything,' he said curtly. 'In fact, a moment ago I seem to recall you dismissed my sister's request as melodramatic nonsense.'

Joanna's chin lifted. 'Look, Mr Anstey, if you mean to be unpleasant there's no point in going on with this.'

He controlled himself with visible effort. 'I'm sorry. This isn't easy for either of us. Believe me, the last thing I wanted was to come barging in on you tonight, of all nights. But I've got so little time to get things settled.' One black eyebrow lifted. 'And I assumed you'd need the will. It seemed best to get it over with. Not best for you, nor for me, but for Polly.' He smiled wryly at her questioning look. 'Her favourite song, "Polly Wolly Doodle". The name stuck.'

'I see.' Joanna looked at her watch, then over at the car. 'Are you driving back to London now?'

'No. I haven't slept much lately. I couldn't face the drive back to town tonight. On the way here I booked a room at the Lamb and Flag in the village. The landlady's organising some supper, after which my plan is to tuck Polly up in one bed and crash out in the other myself.'

'I see.' Joanna braced herself. 'In that case, Mr Anstey, would you consider bringing your— bringing Polly to see me in the morning?'

'On approval, you mean?' he queried scathingly.

'*No!*' Joanna's nails bit into her palms. 'I'd just like to make Polly's acquaintance. I knew your sister quite well at one time, and I liked her very much. But I find it very hard to visualise her as Paul's mistress.' She paused as Marc Anstey winced. 'I'm sorry. What I'm trying to say is that her relationship with Paul won't prejudice me on the subject of her child's welfare. But right now would be a bad time for Polly and me to meet. In the morning she should feel better, and I—well, shall we say I shall have had time to get used to certain aspects of my husband's life unknown to me until today?' She met his black, assessing eyes candidly. 'I'm not saying I'll do what your sister wanted. For one thing, Polly might hate the sight of me. But what I am saying is that I won't dismiss the idea out of hand.'

'No.' He showed strong white teeth in a mirthless smile. 'Because if you do you lose your money and your house.'

Joanna gave him a patronising little smile. 'As it happens, I don't, Mr Anstey. The house is mine. I was born here. And with care I can continue to live here. I don't need money. Your blackmail wouldn't have worked.'

For a moment Marc Anstey was silent, then he gave her a mocking little bow. 'I apologise, Mrs Clifford. I got the facts wrong.'

'And you a journalist—how *very* strange!'

He threw up a hand, smiling faintly. 'All right, Mrs Clifford. I'll bring Polly here after breakfast in the morning. Just for a few minutes. But she's a little human being, remember, not a puppy. If you do take her you can't send her off to the dogs' home if it doesn't work out.'

Only the memory of a small, tear-stained face prevented Joanna from slamming the door in his face. 'I won't bother to answer that, Mr Anstey. I'll see you at ten in the morning.'

A disquieting gleam flashed in the dark eyes for an instant before Marc Anstey turned away. He paused under the portico light to look at her. 'By the way, I should have said this before. Please accept my condolences. Belated, I'm afraid. If you find it hard to think of Rosa as Paul Clifford's mistress, I find it damned impossible to think of you as his wife.'

'But I'm not his wife, Mr Anstey. I'm his widow. Goodnight.'

Which, thought Joanna, as she bolted the door yet again, was about right. After the revelations of the day it was difficult to remember she'd ever been Paul Clifford's wife. Rosa Anstey and Polly had probably seen far more of Paul than she had during the entire duration of her marriage.

Jim rang later to say his wife's leg was in plaster, and other than feeling mad with herself for doing something so stupid Maisie was in good heart. 'How are you, love?' he asked.

'Like Maisie, as well as can be expected. Give her my love and tell her I'll visit her.' Joanna paused, then told him about the unexpected visitor who'd brought the missing will. 'So I know about the child now, Jim. Paul's left everything to the daughter I never knew he possessed.' She gave a mirthless little laugh. 'He left me the Stubbs painting. You know the one, a grey rather like my poor Saladin. Liked his joke, did Paul.'

Jim groaned. 'I kept trying to tell you about the little girl, love,' he said, 'then the shock about Maisie sent everything out of my head. How do you feel about it?'

'I'll let you know when I've had time to get used to the idea.' She explained about the terms of the will and Rosa Anstey's dying wish regarding her child.

'You've got to be joking!' said Jim, flabbergasted. 'She couldn't have known what she was saying.' He paused. 'I've never met this brother of hers. Heard of him, mind. A bit of a high-flyer, tipped for the top, so I hear. A kid could cramp his style. He might be trying to pull a fast one, Jo, dumping the kid on you to evade his own responsibility.'

'No,' said Joanna, thinking it over. 'I don't think so. In fact, Jim, I rather got the impression that the high-flying Mr Anstey isn't in the least keen to hand his niece over to me. Which is natural enough. He knows nothing about me, after all.'

Jim cleared his throat noisily, sounding embarrassed. 'But Rosa did, love. She admired you no end. I know for a fact she felt pretty bad about what happened with you and Paul. It might seem crazy, but she must have really believed you were the best one to look after her child.'

'She may have,' said Joanna sharply. 'It doesn't mean I'm going to, though, Jim.'

'No, no, of course not.' Jim paused. 'But if this Anstey chap kicks up rough about the will it's going to make things a bit difficult for us all at PCP.'

*   *   *

Joanna went early to bed, but not to sleep. She lay tossing and turning all night, certain she must be insane even to contemplate taking Rosa's child. But the small, tear-stained face of Polly Anstey kept rising to haunt her, along with harrowing thoughts of a dying woman's plea. If she refused to take the child, Joanna had a sinking feeling she'd regret it for the rest of her life.

She smiled bitterly as she realised that Paul had achieved his family in the end, after all, though not in the precise way he'd wanted it. Paola Anstey's great drawback in his eyes would have been her sex. Paul had been so desperate for a son. Joanna shook her head in the darkness, marvelling at her husband's talent for deception. Paul Clifford had lived a lie for years, juggling two separate lives with the skill of a magician. If he hadn't been killed she might never have known. Suddenly Joanna felt a searing pang of inadequacy, depressed at the lack in herself which had sent her husband into the arms of another woman. She wept a few bitter tears into her pillow, then pulled herself together, sniffing, knowing full well she was weeping from wounded pride, rather than grief.

The tears disappeared altogether when Joanna finally acknowledged the inescapable fact that Polly Anstey's pathetic little face was not the only one keeping her awake. As the night wore on she found it harder and harder to dismiss Marc Anstey's dark, haggard features from her mind. Joanna heaved over on to her back restlessly, assuring herself it was only natural to feel *some* sympathy for Marc Anstey. And not for *him* exactly, but for his dilemma. His sister had left him in a pretty pickle

one way and another. Joanna's lip trembled. It
wasn't fair of Rosa to make her feel guilty like this.
Why should she be expected to take charge of
another woman's child? Why had Rosa thought she
could solve her problem by passing it on to Joanna
Clifford? Only the problem wasn't an 'it'. It was a
desolate little girl, crying for her mother. And
probably for her father, too.

Joanna stared miserably at the ceiling, watching
the changes of light as clouds played tag with the
moon outside. Why me? she thought for the hun-
dredth time. Were there no suitable relatives? And,
even if there weren't, surely there was enough
money from the sale of PCP to provide the child
with suitable care? But Rosa had evidently wanted
more than that. She'd wanted Paul's wife to take
over responsibility for his child. Which was
madness. How did she know Joanna Clifford
wouldn't make Polly's life a misery? Unless she'd
instructed her brother to make regular inspections,
satisfy himself that Polly was being treated properly.
It all seemed very unlikely—Joanna lay suddenly
still. Unless, of course, Paul had told Rosa about
the accident.

Joanna got up very early next morning, had a
hot bath, dithered for a while, then pulled on a
scarlet sweater with the same faded Levis of the
night before. Feeling on edge and irritable, she
passed the time until ten by making muffins, wondering if they were the sort of thing little girls liked.
She fidgeted about, tidying up, arranging and re-
arranging sprays of leaves in a copper jar, until by
the time her visitors were due Joanna's nerves were
as taut as piano-wire.

Pulling herself together impatiently, she ran upstairs to brush her hair. She eyed her reddened eyelids and pale face, then shrugged and went downstairs. Marc Anstey could take her as she was.

She was at the window when the car turned into the drive. Prey to a sharp attack of nerves, she opened the door and stood under the portico as Marc Anstey, still in his formal suit, helped a small girl from the car and led her towards the house.

Sleeping, Polly had looked like a sad little angel. Awake and unwilling, she was a sturdy little creature with bright black eyes in a round face still blotchy from weeping, her dark curls untidy. She wore navy shorts and a white T-shirt and clung to her uncle's hand, shrinking against him as he tried to pull her forward. Something eased inside Joanna as she realised that together Marc and Paola Anstey could have been taken for father and daughter. The child bore no resemblance at all to Paul Clifford.

'Hello,' she called casually.

'Good morning,' said Marc Anstey, picking up his niece bodily. 'This is very kind of you, Mrs Clifford. You must excuse Polly. She's in a very unsociable mood.'

'Never mind. Come in and have some coffee. I'm dying for some.' Joanna led them to the bright, cheerful kitchen, waving Marc to a chair at the table. He set Polly on his knee, where she snuggled against him, thumb in mouth, her eyes fixed on Joanna.

All fingers and thumbs under the black, unblinking scrutiny, Joanna made coffee and carried a tray to the table, then sat down in a chair opposite her visitors, smiling brightly.

'How was breakfast at the Lamb and Flag?'

'Difficult.' Marc sighed wearily as he shifted the child more comfortably on his lap. 'Polly wasn't in an eating mood. And after twenty minutes of intensive coaxing neither was I.'

Joanna poured hot, strong coffee into two tall mugs, then looked enquiringly at the child. 'How about you, Polly? Do you like coffee?'

No response.

'Milk? Orange juice?'

A flicker of interest lit the dark eyes. Taking it for assent, Joanna poured juice from a carton into a beaker and set it within the child's reach.

'I don't suppose you'd fancy a muffin, Mr Anstey?' she asked casually.

Marc Anstey's eyes brightened. 'English muffins? Wonderful! I haven't tasted one in years.'

Battening down the hatches on her emotions, Joanna applied herself to toasting and buttering. She kept up a light, superficial conversation with Marc Anstey, making no attempt to talk to the little girl as she handed out plates and napkins. Marc Anstey polished off two muffins at flattering speed, while Polly, finding no one was taking any notice of her, warily tasted the fragment of muffin her uncle tossed on her plate for her to try.

'I like it,' she said in a hoarse, weary little voice.

Joanna smiled. 'Good. Shall I toast a fresh one for you?'

Polly nodded mutely, then as Marc sent her a meaning look she muttered, 'Yes, please.'

While the adults drank more coffee the child ate her muffin to the last crumb, then drank a second beaker of orange juice.

'The catering seems more popular here than the Lamb and Flag,' said Marc lightly, then gave Joanna a significant look. 'We must be going soon.'

'Not yet!' Joanna looked up with a smile of relief as Doris arrived. 'Morning, Doris. This is Mr Marc Anstey, and the lady on his knee is Polly.'

'Pleased to meet you,' said Doris, beaming at the little girl.

Polly favoured Doris with one of her unwinking scrutinies, then her orange-rimmed mouth curved in a faint suggestion of a smile. She slid down from her uncle's knee. 'Loo, please,' she said imperiously.

Doris held out her hand. 'Right you are, young miss. Will you come with me?'

Polly nodded serenely, surrendered her hand to the firm, rough grasp, and trotted off without a backward glance.

Joanna looked at Marc in astonishment. 'Well!'

'Three cheers for Doris.' He leaned forward, his face suddenly urgent. 'Look, since we're out of Polly's earshot so unexpectedly, can you tell me how you feel now you've met her? Or is it too soon?'

She looked at him, defeated. 'I lay awake all night wrestling with my conscience.'

He tensed, his face colourless with strain. 'And?'

'I decided the best thing was to have Polly to stay for a day or two before we come to any hasty decisions.'

Marc's eyes narrowed. 'It could mean quite a hold-up for the sale of PCP.'

Joanna's eyes smouldered. 'Mr Anstey, you can do whatever you like with Polly's inheritance. As I told you last night, I don't need——' She bit her

lip, as it suddenly occurred to her that if she had
a child to bring up and educate this was not exactly
true.

'If you do take Polly,' he said swiftly, 'provision—generous provision—would be made for
her, and for you.'

They looked at each other in silence for a
moment, then Joanna nodded reluctantly. 'I'd have
to accept it, for Polly's sake—*if* she stays with me.'
She eyed him curiously. 'Mr Anstey, what I find so
extraordinary is that you don't have anyone else
who could take Polly.'

'If I had, do you think I'd have come to you,
Mrs Clifford?' He turned away, grimacing. 'I'm
sorry. I could have put that more gracefully. What
I mean is that our parents are dead, Rosa and I the
only children. My father's family washed their
hands of him when he married the orphaned Sicilian
girl he found wandering the streets of Naples towards the end of the war. I do have relatives, yes.
But I've never met any of them, nor do I wish to.'
He swung round suddenly. 'And you know Paul
had no one, either. Or no one he'd admit to.'

Joanna's eyes narrowed. Something in his tone
suggested Marc Anstey and Paul Clifford had never
been soul-mates.

'Nevertheless, Mr Anstey, I'm still surprised that
your sister thought *I*'d take Polly.'

Marc Anstey's black eyes shuttered. 'If you want
the truth, Mrs Clifford, I'll give you her reasons
verbatim—even at the risk of alienating you completely. Rosa said you lost a child, and couldn't have
any more. She seemed to think that by handing
Paul's daughter over to you she was making up for

that. I thought it was a lousy idea. But I couldn't say so—not when it was damn near the last thing I was ever going to say to her.' He swallowed convulsively and turned away, his fists clenched at his side.

Joanna's hand went out to him, then dropped hastily as Doris ushered in a washed and tidied Polly. Joanna's heart contracted at the tenderness in Marc Anstey's smile as he greeted the little girl.

'Polly would like a walk in the garden,' announced Doris. 'Is it all right if I take her round the stables, Mrs Clifford?'

'You'd like that, Polly?' asked Joanna.

The child nodded vigorously. She went off with Doris, chattering in a hoarse little voice, leaving Joanna with a wistful feeling she identified with some surprise. She wanted Polly's approval, too.

'Are the stables in use?' asked Marc.

Joanna began clearing away, her back to him. 'No. Not any more.'

'It was you who used to ride, I take it. I can't see Paul on a horse.'

She shot him a glance over her shoulder. 'You obviously disliked Paul.'

One shoulder lifted in a very Latin shrug. 'Not exactly. I disapproved.'

'Because of Rosa?'

'Exactly.' He smiled without mirth. 'Most of the time I behave like your average Brit, but the Sicilian in me rose up in revolt when Paul Clifford set my sister up as his mistress.'

'An old-fashioned word.'

'Rosa *was* old-fashioned. She never looked at another man from the first day she went to work for Paul Clifford. He was the one great love of her life.' One black eyebrow rose sardonically. 'I don't think he felt the same about her, by any means.'

Joanna turned to face him. 'Since she gave him a child I imagine he cared for her a lot. Paul wanted a family very much.'

Marc examined his fingernails intently. 'Polly owes her existence to the fact that it was Rosa whom Paul turned to when you lost *your* child. She offered comfort, and because she'd been in love with him for years the inevitable happened. They became lovers. She became pregnant.'

'Whereupon Paul moved her into the Chelsea house and engaged a new secretary.' Joanna tried to smile and failed. 'From then on my marriage was virtually over. When Paul learned I couldn't have any more children, I think——' She thought for a moment. 'I think Paul felt cheated. As though he'd made a bad bargain.'

'Bargain?'

Joanna nodded. 'He made it possible for me to keep this house. In return I married him and promised to provide him with children.'

Marc frowned. 'Did you love him?'

'I thought I did. I wouldn't have married him otherwise. I'd just lost my father, and Paul—well, I suppose I looked on Paul as the ideal person to take his place. But I was never *in* love with Paul. He was twenty years older than me. In the beginning the gap didn't seem to matter. He——' she stopped, flushing.

'Enjoyed having a young, beautiful bride,' said Marc drily.

Her eyes frosted over. 'Quite so. Perhaps we should go outside. No doubt you'll want to satisfy yourself that my house and garden are suitable as a home for Polly.'

He nodded distantly. 'Thank you—Mrs Clifford.'

They went out into the damp, misty morning to find Polly helping Doris pick blackberries from the thornless bushes in the orchard beyond the stables. She ran to Marc, flushed and very different from the woebegone child of earlier on.

'Marco! Look—they've got apples on trees here!'

He laughed and picked her up, kissing her cheek. 'Of course they do, you little townie.'

'Can we stay to lunch?' demanded the child.

Marc shook his head. 'We ought to be going.'

'Would you like to stay, Polly?' asked Joanna.

Polly nodded, smiling at Joanna for the first time. 'Yes.'

'Please!' prompted Marc.

The child repeated it obediently, wriggling to get down.

'I'm helping Doris,' she said importantly. She ran off without a backward glance, leaving a strained silence behind her.

'She seems to like it here,' said Marc, as he strolled with Joanna towards the stables.

'I hope so.'

'When shall I leave her with you?'

Joanna opened the top half of one of the doors, gazing into the empty manger. 'Whenever suits you, Mr Anstey.'

He was silent for a moment, leaning beside her. 'I'm due back in Washington next week. If I brought Polly here the day after tomorrow, I could put up in the Lamb and Flag for a couple of days, stay within reach in case——'

'I'm beating her regularly?'

'No,' he said wearily. 'In case I'm needed. If the arrangement doesn't work I'll just have to engage a full-time nanny and find a bigger flat.'

Joanna thought about it in silence. If Marc Anstey was on hand for a time at the beginning it might ease the initial stages of her relationship with Polly. As yet the little girl was far more taken with Doris than her dead father's wife. Joanna squared her shoulders.

'All right. Let's do that.'

Marc turned to her. 'Are you sure?'

'Yes.'

He held out his hand formally. 'Let's shake on it, then.'

Joanna smiled coolly and put her hand in his for an instant, then detached her fingers hastily, horrified to find her pulse racing at his touch. She turned back to the empty stable, saying the first thing that came into her head. 'I had a horse called Saladin who used to live in here.'

'Did you sell him?'

'No. Paul had him destroyed.'

Marc shot a startled glance at her. 'Why?'

'I had a fall when I was riding him. It was my fault, not Saladin's. But I lost the baby. Paul went berserk, took his anger and disappointment out on the horse. I was told I'd have miscarried anyway, fall or no fall, but by the time I was discharged from the hospital Saladin was dead.'

They stared into the dark stable for some time in silence.

'Couldn't you have bought another horse?' Marc asked at last.

'No.' Joanna cleared her throat. 'Paul held the purse-strings. I had no money of my own.'

Marc Anstey turned to watch his niece running about on the grass in the distance. 'Couldn't you have got a job—earned some money of your own?'

The open disapproval in his tone stung Joanna. 'That's a very personal remark! As it happens I did find a way to earn money. Eventually. But not enough for luxuries like horses.' She paused, shaken to find herself so angry. 'Mr Anstey, I think we should get certain things straight. The only thing you and I have in common is Polly. You have my assurance that if she stays with me I'll do my utmost to give her a good home and make her happy. But I want everything legally sorted out beforehand, including your rights where she's concerned— reasonable access and so on. Beyond that, you and I need have nothing to do with each other.'

Marc Anstey said something under his breath, a leap of dislike in his eyes as they clashed with hers. 'Rosa was wrong. This just isn't going to work.'

Joanna shrugged disdainfully. 'I don't see why not. The equation's obvious. Polly lost a mother. I lost a child. I lay awake most of last night thinking it over, and came to the conclusion that Rosa was right. It's the perfect solution.'

He looked at her moodily for a long, tense moment. 'I'll reserve judgement until this trial period's over—but, whichever way things turn out, keep one thing very much in mind,' he added, with sinister emphasis. 'Polly might lack a mother, but she's not alone in the world. Anyone who harms a single hair of her head will have me to contend with. And I can fight dirty, Mrs Clifford. Believe me.'

CHAPTER THREE

JOANNA'S home was late Georgian, quite small, and classically simple in design. A single pillar supported the porch. Above it a half-moon window formed a pleasing note of contrast among the oblong sash windows flanking the main door of Swan House, which stood in three acres of land mainly given over to woodland and orchard. As a child Joanna had run free there with her friends, and was convinced that in time Polly could be just as happy in the same surroundings.

But much as she loved her home, the day Joanna was expecting Marc Anstey with Polly it felt like a cage. After her sudden tirade at the stable door Marc had called his niece to him and taken her away at once, deaf to the child's pleas to stay for lunch, and Joanna's last view of Polly had been a forlorn little hand waving from the back window of the car. Marc Anstey had made it plain that diplomatic relations between himself and Paul Clifford's widow were at an end. Not, Joanna assured herself, that she minded. Her view of the entire male sex was somewhat jaundiced after her experience with Paul.

As the time grew closer to Polly's arrival Joanna began to get cold feet, more convinced by the minute that she'd been mad even to think of trying to bring up someone else's child. It wasn't as if she had experience of motherhood in any form herself.

Her own mother had taken off with a lover before her daughter could walk, leaving Joanna to the loving but eccentric care of a father who looked on dogs, horses, music and literature as the only necessities in life other than food. Urged by relatives to send his child away to school, Richard Swan had refused point-blank. In his view the local schools and his own efforts could provide his child with all the education necessary right up to university entrance, and his pleasure was enormous when Joanna proved him right by gaining a first-class degree in art history.

Joanna smiled wryly. Instead of art history and her subsequent secretarial course she'd have done better to train as a nanny for her present undertaking.

She tensed as she heard a car crunch to a halt on the gravel outside. When the bell rang she made herself wait for a moment or two, then opened the door, her smile of welcome fading when she found Marc Anstey alone, looking even more haggard than before.

'Good morning, Mr Anstey,' she said formally. 'Where's Polly?'

'Good morning, Mrs Clifford.' He shrugged, nodding in the direction of the car. 'She fell asleep on the way down. I thought we might have a word out here before I wake her up.'

'By all means.'

He thrust his hands into his pockets, eyeing her warily. 'I suppose I should have rung. To ask if you'd changed your mind.'

Joanna looked past him towards the row of wall-flowers she'd planted on the day Paul died. 'I never change my mind once it's made up.'

'I admire your certainty.'

'Obstinacy, my father called it.'

His eyes, black-ringed with weariness, studied her coolly. 'You were pretty frank last time I was here—regarding any personal dealings between you and me. So I've a suggestion to make.'

'I'm listening,' said Joanna, who had regretted her outburst almost the moment it was made.

'Do you have a solicitor?' he asked.

'I generally leave money matters to Jim Fowler, Paul's financial adviser. He's an old friend.'

Marc nodded. 'I've already been in contact with him over the will. Would he agree to a meeting between the three of us? In the role of Polly's trustee I'd like some kind of contract drawn up and ratified, with your role—and mine—clearly defined where my niece is concerned.'

'I'll arrange it,' said Joanna promptly. 'If he can get down here this evening perhaps the three of us can thrash it out over dinner.'

'Are you asking me to break bread with you, Mrs Clifford?' he asked drily. 'I thought personal contact was to be minimal.'

Joanna's chin lifted. 'Mr Anstey, I'm sorry I was so outspoken the other day. My—my emotions were still pretty raw right then. I've had time to think since, and I realise that it would be very bad for Polly if you and I remain hostile to each other.'

'*You* were hostile, Mrs Clifford, not me.'

Joanna fought down her resentment. 'And I'm trying hard not to be now,' she said tightly. 'What

I'm saying is, shall we start again? If not as friends, at least as two people prepared to make the best of a difficult situation.'

'I'll go for that.' Marc Anstey gave her a faint smile which metamorphosed almost at once into a mammoth yawn.

'You look tired,' commented Joanna.

'Polly wakes up in the night crying for her mother.' He shot a sombre look at her. 'Will you be able to cope with that?'

Joanna ignored a sudden rush of panic. 'I'll do my utmost to cope, I promise. I know none of it will be easy, Mr Anstey——'

'It might be just a bit easier if you call me Marc.'

'All right. You know I'm Joanna.'

'Yes. I know.'

There was a pause while each took stock of the other. Then Marc gave her a twisted smile. 'A shame we had to meet under such bloody awful circumstances.'

'Amen to that,' agreed Joanna bleakly. 'Shall we get Polly out of the car?'

After her nap Polly was sleepy and irritable until she realised she was back in the house with the orchard. The discovery smoothed over the initial stages as the child ran through the house and out into the garden to play there for a while before lunch.

'Does this mean I'm bidden to two meals today?' enquired Marc suavely, eyeing the three places laid at the kitchen table.

Joanna turned away to take hot rolls from the oven. 'I haven't contacted Jim yet. Dinner tonight depends on him.'

Lunch was a difficult meal. Polly, deeply disappointed because Doris was missing, refused to eat more than a spoonful or two of the vegetable soup, which she pronounced different from the soup Mamma made.

'Will Mamma make soup in heaven?' she asked Marc, who looked as though he'd been kicked in the stomach.

'Of course she will, *cara*,' he said gruffly. A pulse throbbed at the corner of his mouth as he fed her a morsel of hot buttered roll. 'The angels will love Mamma's soup. Not,' he added hastily, 'that Joanna's soup isn't delicious.'

Joanna smiled brightly. 'Just different,' she agreed. 'You wouldn't have any recipes, I suppose?'

'Don't worry. It might be best to do your own thing right from the start.'

After lunch the moment Joanna had been dreading came all too soon. Marc, obviously ready to drop, said goodbye to Polly before departing for a rest in his room at the Lamb and Flag. The little girl stared at him incredulously, tears welling up in her dark eyes.

'Want to come too!' she clamoured hoarsely, clinging to his hand like grim death. '*Marco*——'

'No, Polly,' he said coaxingly. 'You stay here with Joanna. I'll see you later. I promise.'

The ensuing scene was every bit as bad as Joanna had feared. Worse, she thought in desperation, as she hung on to a hysterical little girl once Marc

Anstey had torn himself away, his face pale and drawn as he gunned his car down the drive.

Joanna managed to get the screaming, kicking child indoors, then struggled upstairs with her to a small bedroom at the back of the house. She sat down on the bed with the distraught child in her arms, rocking Polly back and forth, murmuring soothing, wordless noises of comfort for a very long time before the exhausted child lapsed into normal tears. Her head burrowed against Joanna's shoulder at last as she wept, the small body shaken by the occasional hiccup as the storm of weeping gradually died away. Joanna, utterly shattered, smoothed a trembling hand over the tangled black curls, her other arm holding Polly close. At last she turned the swollen, forlorn face up to hers and smiled tenderly.

'Polly. I want you to listen to me.'

She felt the little body tense.

'I used to know your Mamma quite well,' Joanna began with care. 'So before Mamma had to go to heaven, she asked your Uncle Marc——'

'Marco,' corrected Polly hoarsely.

Joanna bit her lip. 'Right. Marco. She asked him to give you to me to look after.'

A quiver ran through the small body. 'Why?' demanded Polly.

'Because I don't have a little girl, you see. Your Mamma knew I wanted one. So she gave you to me. Won't you stay with me so I won't be lonely any more?'

'Marco too?' asked Polly hopefully.

Joanna blinked. 'Your uncle's job means he has to be in America a lot, so he can't *live* here. But he can come and see you whenever he wants, I promise. Look. Cross my heart!'

Polly's forehead creased in a frown while her dazed little mind grappled with the new idea. Joanna waited, tense, then at long last the curly black head nodded slowly, one small shoulder lifting in exact imitation of her uncle.

'Suppose so,' said Polly listlessly, then brightened. 'Doris? Will I see Doris if I live with you?'

'Most days,' Joanna promised. 'She helps me with the house.'

Polly sat up, beginning to take in her surroundings. Her eyes went from the pictures of Winnie-the-Pooh on the wall, to the row of battered teddy bears sitting on a shelf, then opened saucer-wide as they saw the doll's house in the corner. 'Does a little girl live here?'

Joanna let Polly get down to explore. 'Not now. This used to be my room when I was a little girl like you.'

Polly looked surprised. 'Yours?'

'Yes. If you open that chest over there you'll find more toys. They used to be mine, but you can have them now. If you like,' added Joanna casually.

But Polly wasn't listening. Her attention was riveted on the large Victorian doll's house filled from kitchen to attic with miniature nineteenth-century furniture. She turned to Joanna in wonder. 'Yours, too?'

'Yes. My daddy made it for me.'

Polly looked wistful. 'I haven't got a daddy.'

Joanna's heart stood still. 'Haven't you, darling?'

'No. Only Marco—and Uncle Paul.'

Joanna swallowed. 'Uncle Paul?'

Polly nodded absently, her attention on the wonders of the doll's house. 'He came to our house a lot. But he's gone to heaven now too.'

Deciding it was dangerous to continue the conversation without advice from Marc Anstey, Joanna showed Polly how to unfasten the wall of the doll's house to reveal the rooms inside. 'Would you like to play up here for a minute while I make a telephone call?'

'Can I take out the dollies?' entreated Polly.

'Yes, of course. Only they like to go back in their places afterwards. When I come back I'll tell you their names, if you like.'

The child nodded fervently, then turned back to the house, her small hands reverent as she lifted the baby doll out of the cradle.

Joanna flew to her bedroom and whisked her wedding photograph into a drawer. Then she went systematically through the entire house, removing what few traces of Paul she could find. Her relationship with Polly was likely to be so fragile and difficult for a while that she had no intention of allowing Paul to make life any more difficult than he had already, for Polly's sake as well as her own.

Afterwards Joanna rang Jim Fowler to ask him to dinner. He promised to be with her by eight after he'd been to visit his wife in the hospital.

'What's up, Jo?' he asked uneasily. 'Anstey kicking up rough?'

'No. He just wants everything on a legal footing. I think it's a good idea,' she added firmly. 'See you tonight, Jim.'

She rang the Lamb and Flag, left a message to the effect that the appointment Mr Anstey required had been made, then went back to Polly to suggest they unpack Polly's belongings and put them away.

'Tell you what,' said Joanna. 'Once we've done that I'll take the doll's house down to the kitchen and put it on the table there if you like. I've got a friend coming to dinner, your uncle too, so I've got to get busy.'

Polly assented rapturously, trotting back and forth industriously as they put her clothes away. Joanna's heart contracted as she hung up little dresses exquisitely smocked and embroidered by a loving hand that could only have belonged to Rosa. When everything was put away and a long-maned lion lay on the bed guarding Polly's pyjamas, Joanna took the little girl on a tour of the upper floor, ending with one of the bathrooms, where Polly needed only a little assistance before they went back to collect the doll's house.

Later, as rain lashed against the kitchen windows, Joanna was conscious of an unexpected feeling of peace as she glanced across at the absorbed child from time to time. As she made her preparations for dinner it occurred to her that fate had given her a child of Paul's after all. But in the last way she would have wished.

Once the vegetables were done and the pork tenderloin stood absorbing its flavours of garlic and mustard, ready to cook later, Joanna sat down at the kitchen table to tell Polly the names the youthful Joanna had given her dolls. To a child of the nineties some of the names were very funny. When Polly laughed Joanna rejoiced. If Polly could laugh now and then things wouldn't be too bad. Not, she thought, that she had any delusions about being a substitute for Rosa Anstey. Nor had she any intention of trying to take Rosa's place, even if such a thing were possible. It was essential that she create a role of her own where Polly was concerned.

The first argument arose over the subject of supper. None of Joanna's suggestions appealed to Polly in the slightest.

'You must eat,' said Joanna briskly. 'You hardly had any lunch.'

'Not hungry,' Polly said.

Joanna shrugged. 'OK.'

Polly, plainly expecting to be coaxed, looked taken aback. Her eyes were baffled as Joanna dropped the subject and helped her put all the dolls back in their places in their house.

'Bathtime now,' announced Joanna.

'Don't want a bath,' said Polly, eyeing her.

Joanna returned the bright black stare serenely. 'You can go without supper if you like, Polly, but in my house you can't go without a bath. Only clean little girls sleep in my beds. OK?'

Something in Joanna's manner decided Polly not to argue. She sighed gustily. 'OK.'

Matters improved slightly at bathtime, where a flotilla of battered rubber ducks were produced to liven the proceedings. Afterwards, when the little figure was clean and cosy in pyjamas and dressing-gown, her black curls gleaming, Polly unbent towards Joanna sufficiently to confide that her teddy's name was Benno and her pyjama-case was Leone.

'Uncle Paul gave him to me,' she announced as they went downstairs, hand in hand.

Joanna's stomach lurched. 'That's nice. Now, if you don't fancy supper, how about a glass of milk instead?'

Polly, however, had changed her mind. If she could have scrambled eggs on toast she would have some supper.

'Done!' said Joanna.

With delicious smells coming from the oven, the radio playing music softly in the background, the kitchen was a bright, welcoming place as Polly ate her supper with a speed which showed a hunger she'd been determined to hide. She was halfway through a large bowl of ice-cream when her uncle arrived.

'Good evening.' Marc Anstey's smile was a little crooked as Joanna opened the door, his eyes on the smear of flour on her cheek.

'You're early,' she said shortly, wishing she'd thought to remove her striped butcher's apron before letting him in.

'I thought you might need a hand with Polly.' He stopped in the kitchen doorway as a small projectile hurtled across the room and into his arms.

'Marco, Marco, she's got a doll's house—over there—look! She did scrambled egg for me and she made me have a bath but there were ducks——'

'Steady!' laughed Marc, looking vastly relieved. 'What a time you've had, *tesoro*. But it's not good manners to say "she" all the time.' He raised an eyebrow in Joanna's direction. 'How would you like Polly to address you?'

'Joanna?' She smiled a little. 'Or Jo, perhaps. My friends call me that.'

Marc held Polly away from him a little. 'How about it, Polly Wolly Doodle? Are you Joanna's friend? Will you call her Jo?'

Polly cast a thoughtful glance in Joanna's direction, then nodded. 'Jo.' She smiled graciously.

Marc cuddled the curly head against his shoulder, his eyes questioning as he looked at Joanna. 'All right?' he asked softly.

She nodded. 'I think so. Drink?'

The scene in the kitchen could have been any one of thousands like it all over the country at that time of night. The child finishing her supper, the lady of the house preparing dinner, the man of the house just returned from his day in the outside world.

Joanna smiled in secret amusement as she handed Marc a glass of wine.

His eyebrows rose as he thanked her. 'Our acquaintance is short, I know, but I think that's the first smile you've managed other than the lady-of-the-manor social variety.'

Joanna turned away to check on the apples simmering on the hob set into the pine counter. 'It just struck me how strange this is. A few days ago the three of us had never laid eyes on each other. Now——'

'Now here we are, the perfect picture of domesticity!'

'To the casual observer only,' said Joanna tartly.

Marc took a suddenly sleepy Polly on his knee and held her close, his eyes on Joanna over the dark curls. 'Funny, really, you're not in the least what I expected.'

'You can't have known much about what *to* expect, surely!'

'My sister talked about you a great deal.' He looked away. 'Rosa suffered agonies of guilt where you're concerned.'

Joanna winced. 'I'd rather not talk about—about that, please.'

His head swivelled, his eyes holding hers. 'You mean we just shut the past away and pretend she— and your husband—never existed?'

'Not exactly.' Joanna looked at the now sleeping child closely. 'If the little one wants to talk about her mother we'll talk. As much as she wants. But what do I do about Paul? I'm terrified of putting my foot in it with Polly,' she whispered urgently.

Marc nodded, comprehending. 'Show me where to put Polly to bed, then we'll sort a few things out before Fowler gets here.'

The wear and tear on Polly's emotions over the previous few days had finally taken their toll. When Joanna conducted Marc to the small bedroom overlooking the orchard the child was too deeply asleep to stir when he slid her beneath the covers. He tucked Polly's teddy in beside her then stood looking down at the flushed, sleeping face for a moment before following Joanna from the room.

'If we leave the door ajar we'll hear if she cries,' said Joanna, then paused at the head of the stairs. 'Dinner's well in hand. Would you go down to the drawing-room, help yourself to a drink while I tidy myself up? I shan't be long.'

While Marc went downstairs Joanna turned back into Polly's room to move the lamp so that its faint glow was away from the child's face. Her throat tightened as she looked down at the sleeping child, and she turned away blindly, hurrying to take a swift shower and change her clothes. Resisting a surprising urge to dress in something eye-catching, she put on the black dress worn for the funeral, knowing Jim would expect a show of mourning. With sudden distaste she pushed aside the jewellery Paul had bought her. Instead she found a silver filigree butterfly her father had given her years before and pinned it to the severe dress, then made up her face with care and brushed back her heavy hair, securing it at the nape of her neck with a black velvet ribbon.

Marc laid down the daily paper and stood up as she entered the softly lit drawing-room, the appreciation in his eyes very gratifying. 'You look very elegant.'

'Thank you.' Joanna smiled politely. 'I must put my chef's hat on again for a while. Would you care to listen to some music while I put the finishing touches to the meal?'

'No,' he said flatly. 'I prefer to watch you. Even help, if you like.'

Joanna had never been offered help in the kitchen, other than Doris's. Not sure she cared for the idea, nor for Marc Anstey's company while she worked, she found herself flustered by the intent dark eyes which followed every move she made as she set to work.

'Are you sure I can't peel something, or wash dishes?' he asked.

'All done, thanks,' she said, her back to him. 'I did most of it earlier while Polly played with the doll's house.'

There was silence for a while.

'Joanna,' said Marc at last.

She turned. 'Yes?'

'Before we get bogged down in facts and figures with Fowler, I want you to know how much I appreciate what you're doing for Polly.' His eyes held hers. 'I know how hard it must be for you—in the circumstances.'

'It's hard for all of us.' She detached her gaze with effort. 'I just hope it works out well. For Polly, I mean.'

'Children adapt, even to loss.'

'I know.'

'Did *you* lose someone?'

'In a way. My mother left my father before I could walk. She drowned in a sailing accident shortly afterwards with her lover. So I suppose you could say I lost her—or she lost me.'

Marc's eyes softened. 'I see. No wonder you feel sympathy for Polly's situation.'

Joanna shook her head as she began to roll out some suet crust. 'It's much worse for Polly. Rosa was always there for her. I never really knew my mother. My father was the centre of *my* little universe.'

'You still miss him?'

'Yes, all the time. He'd have been a great help with Polly.' Joanna spooned apple slices carefully on to the crust, wrapped it in a cloth and put it in a steamer on the hob.

Marc watched, fascinated. 'What on earth is that?'

'Apple dumpling.' She smiled a little. 'Jim's favourite. If you're chicken you eat cheese instead.'

He grinned back, then sobered. 'Strange. I forget now and then.'

She nodded. 'I know. But life has to go on. Tell me, why does Polly believe Paul was her uncle?'

Rosa Anstey had been surprisingly obstinate on the subject of her child's paternity. Because divorce was out of the question she'd insisted Polly never knew Paul Clifford was her father.

'Would you have wanted to divorce him if you'd known?' added Marc, eyeing her.

'You bet I would! Not that I could have done. Paul was a Catholic.'

'Don't I know it!' he said bitterly. 'It was his alibi for not marrying Rosa. While she, devout Catholic though she was, loved him enough to live in sin. Because believe me, Joanna, it *was* sin to her. Thank God she lived long enough to receive the last rites.' His mouth tightened. 'I'd have hated Rosa to die unshriven.'

Joanna looked sick for a moment. 'Paul did.'

Marc stood up abruptly, his dark face brooding under the bright overhead light. 'I can't pretend to be sorry. I didn't care much for your husband.'

'I could hardly fail to realise that!'

'Would you prefer me to go? I could leave the notes I've made. About the agreement for Polly. I could meet Fowler separately another time.'

Joanna considered him thoughtfully. 'You may as well stay now you're here. I've catered for three.'

He raised an eyebrow. 'Do you *want* me to stay?'

She looked away, conscious suddenly that they were discussing more than a mere invitation to dinner. 'Of course,' she said, deliberately casual. 'I'd like to get everything sorted out tonight if possible.'

Marc resumed his seat, refusing a second glass of wine. 'I'd better keep a clear head. I'm still too tired to risk much alcohol.'

'Have some coffee, then.'

'Good Italian coffee?'

She smiled. 'No. Good Brazilian coffee.'

The tension in the air eased. Joanna filled the cafetière, then left Marc to help himself while she put potatoes to roast.

'I hadn't pictured you as so domesticated,' he said, watching her.

'I'm still surprised you know anything about me at all!'

He smiled wryly. 'Rosa couldn't seem to help talking about you. You impressed her no end. She said you were friendly and warm, but at the same time very British and poised, the end product of an expensive education.'

Joanna chuckled. 'I'm British, certainly. But contrary to Rosa's belief I went to the village school and the local comprehensive, then on to a polytechnic, Mr Anstey. Though I must own up to a quite wonderful private tutor as well. My father did Greats at Oxford and bombarded my youthful brain with as much literature and philosophy as it could absorb, with a fair bit of Greek and Roman history thrown in.'

Marc shook his head sorrowfully. 'While I'm just a humble hack, making a living by my pen.'

'Not the way I heard it,' she said sceptically.

He grinned, changing the subject to comment on the way the kitchen was fitted out. 'It's very state-of-the-art in here. Unlike the rest of the house.'

Paul Clifford had wanted to do over the entire house when they had married, meeting with firm resistance from Joanna, who liked it exactly the way it was. To appease him she had given in over the kitchen. 'I admit it was a bit primitive in here. The cupboards and cooker were ancient so I finally gave

in and let Paul loose in here with his idea of the
country-house kitchen.' She made a face. 'Rather
a contrast to the rest of Swan House.'

'Why the name? I haven't seen any swans about,
unless you're hiding a moat somewhere.'

She looked at him levelly. 'Before I was married
I was Joanna Swan. We Swans have lived here for
two hundred years, good yeomen all.'

Marc Anstey smiled wryly. 'Whereas I spring
from exotic but unknown Sicilian stock mixed with
British die-hard respectability.'

'And Jim Fowler, who's due here any minute, is
a product of London's Docklands—long before it
was fashionable to live there!' Joanna removed her
apron. 'I think we're what we are, not who we are.
Paul could never reconcile himself to that point of
view. He married me in his urge for upward mo-
bility, to become part of a world he felt was different from his own. He was disappointed. All he
achieved was an invitation or two to charity func-
tions and an occasional dinner party with the rector
and his wife—who's my closest friend.' She stopped
suddenly, embarrassed. 'I'm sorry. I don't know
why I'm telling you all this. You can't possibly be
interested in my bizarre marriage.'

Marc moved towards her, holding her eyes with
his. 'On the contrary. The subject interests me very
much indeed——' He broke off as the doorbell put
an end to the oddly intimate little moment. 'Ah.
Your visitor. Time to get down to business.'

CHAPTER FOUR

DINNER with Jim Fowler was more of a strain than
lunch with Polly. Long before it was over Joanna
wished she'd arranged a meeting over morning
coffee instead of a three-course meal. While they
ate it was impossible to get down to business, yet
the very reason for the meeting made polite dinner
conversation uphill work. Joanna was glad when
the time came to take coffee into the drawing-room,
though even then both men leapt simultaneously to
take the tray, like dogs with a bone. When they
finally got down to business the atmosphere was
thick with constraint as they began to discuss the
proposals Marc had ready regarding the small
person of Paola Anstey.

'I am Paola's guardian, of course,' began Marc.

'Legally?' pounced Jim.

Marc looked down his nose at the accountant.
'A year ago my sister called in a solicitor and made
the necessary arrangements.' He reached in an
inside pocket and took out a legal document. 'I
think you'll find it in order.'

Jim studied it swiftly, then handed it to Joanna,
who barely glanced at it before handing it back.

'What prompted your sister to do that?' asked
Jim.

Marc eyed him militantly. 'Why shouldn't she?'

'All I'm saying is that she was relatively young.
At her age women don't generally think of wills

and guardians and so on,' said Jim, making an obvious effort to sound reasonable.

'My sister was Paul Clifford's mistress. To Rosa this was flying in the face of her upbringing and religious beliefs.' Marc's face darkened. 'She made provision for her daughter's future because she was convinced God would punish her sooner or later.'

'But that's ridiculous——' began Jim, then subsided at a searing blue look from Joanna.

'Some people might think Rosa's been proved right,' she reminded him.

'*I* don't,' said Marc bitingly. 'Paul drove like a maniac. *He* killed Rosa, not God.'

The silence following this statement was so unbearable that Joanna rushed to break it. 'Where was Polly when it happened?'

'At home with the woman who came in to help Rosa.' Marc smiled faintly at Joanna. 'Mrs Tucker is a lot like your Doris Mills, by the way. When Rosa failed to appear she contacted me. You know the rest.' Marc breathed in deeply, then laid out a typed list in front of Jim Fowler, who scanned it through his thick-lensed glasses in silence for a while before giving it to Joanna.

'Anyone would think you were doing Joanna a favour by handing the kid over to her,' said Jim, eyeing Marc challengingly. 'It seems to me you get the penny and the bun. You've got the say-so about the child's education and so on, while Jo here gets all the work and responsibility.'

Marc looked dangerous for a moment. 'I know damn well it looks that way, but this wasn't my idea, remember. I'm merely carrying out my sister's dying wishes. I thought it was a crazy idea to ask Mrs Clifford to take my niece. Frankly I expected her to slam the door in my face.'

'What would you have done if she had?' asked Jim promptly.

'Bought a bigger flat and engaged a nanny I could trust Polly to while I'm away. Which I can still do,' Marc added bluntly, 'if the trial period agreed on between Mrs Clifford and myself proves that the arrangement won't work.'

'It will work,' said Joanna. 'After what Polly's been through it must work, for her sake.' She picked up the sheet of regulations. 'Now. You don't say much about education, other than the money available for it, which, incidentally, is more than enough to send her to a very expensive boarding-school.'

Marc nodded. 'But not yet, surely!'

'Of course not yet! But I think I should be allowed an opinion on the choice of school,' said Joanna.

'I should bloody well hope so!' exploded Jim. 'You're the one left holding the baby, my girl.'

'Yes, I know, Jim,' said Joanna patiently. 'This is all very difficult as it is. Let's not make it worse.'

'Sorry, love.' Jim subsided, glaring at Marc.

'The village school here is very good,' said Joanna in a businesslike way aimed at lightening the tension. 'If you're agreeable I'd prefer that Polly start her education there after Christmas. We can leave decisions about other schools until she's older. Much older.'

Relief smoothed some of the lines etched at Marc's mouth and eyes. 'Thank you,' he said quietly. 'I'm grateful.'

'I can do a little extra-curricular coaching myself,' she said, warming to the idea. 'Drawing and reading and so on.'

'What about your own work?' demanded Jim. 'Won't that suffer?'

'I can fit that in around Polly,' said Joanna, unconcerned.

Marc frowned. 'I'd forgotten your job. What exactly do you do?'

'Don't worry. I do it at home.'

'She writes children's books. *And* illustrates them,' said Jim proudly.

Marc eyed Joanna with a hint of accusation in his dark eyes. 'In that case surely Polly will be a hindrance?'

'Probably. But only at first. I'll just organise my day differently, that's all.' She smiled sweetly. 'They're not three-volume novels.'

'Perhaps you'll show me some time.'

'If you like.' Joanna turned back to the agreement. 'Shall we get the rest of this settled, please?'

The other items were routine matters which Jim vetted quickly, agreeing to all the financial arrangements with such readiness that Joanna knew they were generous rather than merely fair. When Marc agreed that the sale of the factory should go through at once the atmosphere between the two men thawed slightly. Then Joanna came across a final item over the page. She read it through twice, her eyes narrowing. She looked up at Marc with sudden hostility.

'I don't care for the tone of this last bit.'

Jim snatched the paper from her, frowning as he read the final clause. 'In the event of Mrs Clifford's remarriage, all the foregoing would be subject to review.' He eyed Marc Anstey belligerently. 'What the hell does that mean?'

'If Mrs Clifford remarries I shall want Polly back in my sole care immediately.'

'Why?' snapped Joanna, her eyes like chips of blue ice.

Marc shrugged. 'Part of the reason Rosa was so desperate for you to have her child was that I'm not married, and the very nature of my job makes it difficult to provide a permanent base for Polly for the time being. Rosa was adamant that a child needs stability as well as love. But I'm damn sure she wouldn't want Polly at the mercy of some step-father figure if you marry again.'

'Did she say so?' demanded Jim.

'She didn't have to!'

'But you've got nothing in writing.'

Marc jumped to his feet. 'Writing or not, those are my conditions, take it or leave it.'

Joanna got up more slowly. 'I need time to think it over. Before I do, may I ask a personal question?'

'Of course.'

'What happens if *you* marry? Will I be expected to hand Polly back?'

He shrugged, a grim little smile playing at the corners of his mouth. 'Marriage is a snare I've done my best to avoid. The situation's unlikely to arise.' He paused, one eyebrow raised in the way Joanna was beginning to know. 'How about you, Mrs Clifford? Have you anyone in mind to replace Paul?'

Joanna waved a furious Jim out of the way. 'No, Mr Anstey, not yet. It's only a few days since he died—not much to cast around for a suitable candidate. I'll let you know the moment I sort one out.' She paused, two spots of colour burning along her cheekbones. 'How about lovers? Am I allowed those?'

His nostrils flared. 'I'm glad you find this all so amusing——'

'On the contrary,' she snapped. 'I don't find it amusing at all!'

'Look here, Anstey——' began Jim heatedly.

'Leave it, Jim,' ordered Joanna. 'I'm determined the trial period will continue as agreed. Discussion over for tonight, if you don't mind, gentlemen.'

Joanna knew perfectly well that Marc Anstey was reluctant to leave at the same time as Jim Fowler, but she made it crystal-clear she was bidding goodnight to both men. Marc was forced to return to the Lamb and Flag without the private word he so clearly wanted.

Joanna, suddenly wakeful after an energetic burst of clearing up after the meal, went upstairs to check that all was well with Polly, then took a bath to calm her anger over the proviso at the end of Marc Anstey's set of rules. It seemed that as long as she remained a widow she was allowed to function as a surrogate mother to Paola Anstey, for which service she would receive an allowance generous enough to render the sale of Swan House unnecessary. Which, of course, was a relief. She hated the thought of losing her home, and as yet her earnings from the series of Snowbird books were not quite enough to banish the spectre altogether. At the same time she had no intention of letting anyone try to run her private life for her, Marc Anstey in particular.

Joanna felt irritated and depressed as she got ready for bed. A few days ago she'd never heard of Marc Anstey, nor of Polly. Yet now both uncle and niece loomed large in her life, an advantage in one way, since it left her precious little time for bitterness and recrimination where Paul was concerned.

She took her wedding photograph from the drawer and stared at it, trying to remember how she'd felt that day five years before. The wedding had been a quiet, private affair, soon after her father's death. Paul, as short of relatives as his bride, had requested as few people as possible. The only guests at the brief ceremony, and at the lunch at the Ritz afterwards, had been Jim and Maisie Fowler. Joanna had felt very much alone without even Mary Lavenham to lend her support. But her staunchest friend, who would otherwise have seen her through thick and thin, had been too close to presenting her husband with twins to act as bridesmaid.

Joanna gazed at the fair, laughing girl in the simple silk suit and tilted hat, and marvelled at her youth. She felt at least a hundred years older now than the Joanna of her wedding day. Paul, maturely handsome in his morning suit, looked triumphant as he grinned at the camera. How pleased he'd been with himself. And with his bride. Yet once

his hope of a family had been snatched from him
all that had died a very sudden death.

The telephone startled Joanna out of her reverie.
She snatched off the receiver, her voice sharp as she
snapped her name.

'Marc Anstey here.'

Joanna frowned. 'Yes? Is something wrong? It's
very late.'

'I know. I'm sorry.' He paused, then said stiffly,
'I offended you this evening. I was rude. I
apologise.'

'I was surprised rather than offended,' she assured him, calm again.

'And very unapproachable. Too much so for me
to ask when I could visit Polly tomorrow.'

'Come whenever you like. But if you want her
full attention I'd make it after lunch. Doris will be
here in the morning.'

'Which brings me to one of the things I meant
to mention tonight. The news about your writing
came as a surprise. If I allot you a larger allowance, would Doris come in every day from now
on to leave you more time for your work?'

'I'd already thought of that. But I don't need
extra money for her wages.'

'You mean you'd rather not accept anything else
from me.'

'But it isn't from you, Mr Anstey, is it? The
money will come from the sale of PCP in Polly's
name.'

'I used the word "allot", not "give",' he pointed
out coldly. 'Thank you. I'll be round about two
tomorrow. If that's convenient.'

'Perfectly. Goodnight.'

Joanna took some time to get to sleep, then woke in the middle of the night, heart pounding and disorientated, to the sound of crying. She slid out of bed to run to Polly's room, where the child lay in a crumpled heap, sobbing, heartbroken, for her mother.

Joanna took the little girl into her arms and held her tightly, waiting patiently for the storm to pass. It was a long time before Polly quietened. At last she yawned widely, then snuggled her head against Joanna with a shuddering sigh.

'Thirsty,' she said hoarsely.

Joanna mopped the sodden little face with a handkerchief, then poured orange juice from the insulated flask she'd filled earlier. Polly drank deeply, consented to a trip to the bathroom, then allowed herself to be tucked back into bed, wide black eyes fixed imploringly on Joanna's.

'Story. Please?'

'All right. Just a little one. I'll tell you about a pony called Snowbird.'

With the hot, damp little hand held tightly in hers Joanna began on the story she'd been working on before Polly's advent. Snowbird was a white pony whose adventures were gratifyingly popular with under-tens both nationwide and overseas. Joanna did full dramatic justice to the latest episode in Snowbird's career, making a mental note of a new twist in the plot as she went along. Polly was fascinated. At first her reddened eyes never left Joanna's face, but as the minutes ticked by her lids began to droop. Joanna's voice grew quieter and quieter until she was sure the child was asleep, then she tiptoed from the room and slid into her own bed with a sigh. Looking after a grieving, motherless little girl promised to be no sinecure. But if Polly wanted to stay at Swan House she was determined to make a success of it. And not for Rosa, either, nor even Marc, but for Polly. And, Joanna realised with sudden insight, for herself, too. Even with all the problems which came as part of the package she knew with sudden conviction that the child was exactly what she needed to fill the aching, empty void in her life.

Joanna woke next morning to see Polly perched on the end of her bed, watching her.

'Good morning, Polly,' she said, yawning, and looked at the clock. 'You're early.'

'Can I come in your bed?'

Joanna smiled drowsily. 'Yes, of course.'

Polly wriggled down under the covers, then turned her face on the pillows towards Joanna. 'What a lovely big bed! Bigger than Mamma's.'

'Is it?'

'Uncle Paul slept in Mamma's bed sometimes.'

Joanna swallowed, suddenly wide awake. 'Really?'

Polly nodded vigorously. 'I didn't go in Mamma's bed when he was there.'

'No room, I expect.'

'Mamma said I mustn't.'

'I see,' said Joanna faintly, and changed the subject. 'What would you like for breakfast?'

The morning went by on wings, due principally to Polly's delight at seeing Doris Mills, who in her usual unfussy style handed the child a duster and enlisted her help. Polly trotted round after her all morning, proudly helping while the day's chores were dispatched with Doris's usual efficiency and speed.

When Marc Anstey arrived, dead on the stroke of two, Polly leapt up into his outstretched arms, burying her head on his shoulder without a word. Joanna looked on in dismay. The morning had gone so smoothly with Doris around she'd expected Polly to greet her uncle with a torrent of excited chatter. Instead the little girl clung to her uncle like a limpet as he carried her in the house.

'Hey,' said Marc teasingly, as he detached Polly's clinging arms to give her a big kiss. 'Aren't you going to say hello?'

'Tell Uncle Marc——' began Joanna.

'Marco!' interrupted Polly peremptorily. 'I *told* you.'

Joanna flushed. 'Tell—tell Marco what you've been doing all morning.'

Polly brightened, her face suddenly animated as she told Marc how she'd helped Doris with the housework. Then Jo had taken her out to explore the stables and she'd helped tidy the little house where Jo's horse used to live.

'*And* I swept the floor, but I got dirty and she— Jo,' added Polly hastily at the look in Marc's eye, 'Jo made me have *another* bath because I got muddy. And I had pancakes for lunch,' she finished triumphantly.

'Lucky old you,' said Marc, smiling. 'I didn't. Now then, the sun's come out, so perhaps the lady of the house will take two townies like us for a walk and show us some of the local countryside.'

Joanna smiled. 'Good idea. Come on, Polly, let's change our shoes.'

'How's she been?' asked Marc later, as Polly ran on ahead through the orchard towards the woods beyond the boundary wall, looking as carefree as though the moment of melancholy had never happened.

'She cried for Rosa in the night. But I expected that.'

'What did you do?'

Joanna eyed him caustically. 'What do you think? I cuddled her and mopped her up and gave her a drink. Then I told her a story. Before it was finished she was asleep.'

Marc lifted a shoulder. 'I wasn't criticising, believe it or not. I just wondered how you felt about coping with a situation that's likely to crop up pretty often for a while. The doctor says she'll adjust in time——'

'Doctor?' Joanna asked swiftly.

Marc nodded as they resumed their progress towards an impatient Polly. 'Before I brought her down I took her to Rosa's GP. He's known Polly from birth. It seemed a good idea to know what shots she's been given and so on, what illnesses she's had. Unfortunately for you, she hasn't had anything much so far except the odd sore throat and a cold or two.'

'Unfortunately for me,' repeated Joanna. 'Does that mean you've made up your mind about leaving her with me then?'

He stopped dead, his hand on her arm. 'Do you still want her?'

'Of course I want her——' Joanna broke off as Polly ran towards her, demanding to know where they were going.

The afternoon was warm, more like summer than the beginning of autumn. Joanna put all her worries firmly from her mind as she took pride in showing off the beauty of her home surroundings to her guests. They crunched their way through woods carpeted with the first multicoloured fall of leaves. Polly paddled happily through them in her green rubber boots, reluctant to leave until Joanna suggested they climb the hill which gave them a view of the village of Swancote below.

When they reached the top, breathless and a little dishevelled after the climb, Marc rested a foot on an outcrop of rock at the summit and leaned forward to look down at the village. 'Is it called Swancote after your family?'

'Locals say so, but I doubt it. More likely to be a corruption of Swinecote, according to George Lavenham, the rector.' Joanna retied the scarf holding her hair in place at the nape of her neck, one eye on Polly, who was clambering happily over a rocky mound behind them, the other on Marc, who looked far more at home in his surroundings than Joanna had expected. The high-flyer in the expensive suit was missing today, replaced by a relaxed man in a suede bomber-jacket and rubbed corduroys, a red handkerchief knotted at the open neck of his shirt. Even his gypsyish black hair and swarthy skin seemed very much in harmony with the patchwork backdrop of woods and fields in the soft, hazy sunshine.

'I feel like a specimen on a slide,' he said in an undertone, so that Polly wouldn't hear. 'Why the analytical look? Am I dressed incorrectly for a stroll in the country?'

'On the contrary,' said Joanna. 'It was Paul——' She stopped, biting her lip.

'Go on,' he prompted. 'Paul what?'

'It seems disloyal to say so, but Paul insisted on wearing a waxed jacket and flat cap if he so much as went outside the door down here.' Joanna shrugged. 'It looked all wrong on him, somehow. Paul was at his best on city pavements—but I shouldn't be saying so.'

'Because he's dead?'

Joanna nodded. 'Yes, because he's dead. And can't defend himself.'

Marc jumped to his feet and held out a hand to Polly. 'Come on, *cara*. Time to go back.'

Polly protested for a while, but, at the promise of more toasted muffins when they reached the house, trotted off happily enough, the other two following a little way behind.

'I leave tomorrow,' said Marc abruptly. 'We need to talk.' He glanced sideways at Joanna. 'I'd like to ask you out to dinner——'

'Not possible, I'm afraid. I'd need a baby-sitter, even if——'

'Even if you wanted to dine with me, which you don't!'

'I didn't say that. And I agree we need to talk.' She hesitated. 'You're welcome to share my supper, if you like. But it won't be anything elaborate tonight.'

He kicked his way through the leaves, his face sombre. 'I could eat at the pub and come back afterwards.'

'As you like,' she said indifferently.

'I don't like,' he said with sudden violence, then checked himself, breathing deeply. 'Look, I don't care a damn what we eat. But I'd like to talk to you without Jim Fowler glowering as if I intended nicking the silver. And I'd like to pay for the meal, organise it. As it is I feel like some bloody gigolo on the make for a rich widow.'

At Joanna's spontaneous giggle Polly turned to come running towards them, attracted by the sound.

'I'm hungry,' she announced.

'Good.' Joanna took her hand, motioning to Marc to take the other. 'Let's see how fast we can run home, then.'

Marc went back to the Lamb and Flag once Polly was in bed and asleep. His male pride appeased by Joanna's offer of bacon and eggs eaten at the kitchen table, he returned to Swan House so quickly that she had barely enough time to get ready before he was back, showered and shaved, and wearing a fresh shirt, but otherwise looking much as he'd done earlier on.

He eyed her well-worn Levis and outsize scarlet sweater with approval. 'Much better. You look approachable like that.'

'It seemed the right outfit for bacon and eggs,' she said lightly, 'but why should it make me more approachable?'

'Last night, in your mourning black, you were very much Paul Clifford's widow.' He strolled after her into the kitchen. 'Tonight it's easier to see the woman behind all that, the one Rosa trusted to take care of Polly.'

'I hope she was right.' Joanna handed him some cutlery and napkins and told him to lay the table. 'Would you like a drink?'

'No, thanks. I must get back to London tonight, ready to tie up a few loose ends in the morning before I go back to Washington. Shall I cut some of this bread?'

'Yes, please. I shan't be long.'

Marc sat in one of the kitchen chairs, watching Joanna as she moved deftly about her lavishly equipped kitchen. 'You like cooking,' he stated.

'Yes. There's something satisfactory about producing an appetising meal.' She slid sausages and several rashers of bacon under the grill then smiled across at him as she sliced mushrooms and tomatoes. 'In my father's opinion, my real preference, degree or no degree, was marriage, a home—preferably this one—plus a couple of children, a dog or two, a horse if I was lucky, and a room to myself to write my great novel. How do you like your eggs?'

'Any way you care to cook them.' He studied her with narrowed eyes. 'But isn't that, more or less, what Paul offered you?'

'I certainly thought so when he proposed.' Joanna turned her back to supervise the food under the grill, then took out a frying-pan for the eggs. 'What I actually got was quite a bit different. Paul made it possible for me to keep the house, of course. But I found he hated dogs. He wouldn't let me look for a job, yet he regarded my Snowbird stories as a waste of time. Until the first one was accepted. He changed his mind then; stopped being so patronising. But I could have coped with all that. The real damage was done because he was so wrapped up in his rage and anguish over the miscarriage that he never gave a thought to the fact that I was suffering too. He left me alone, took off to London, and you know what happened after that.'

Marc looked grim. 'Yes. None better.'

Joanna took warm plates from under the grill and began to serve out their meal, making a face as she eyed the finished results. 'Very definitely not in the health-food bracket, but rather nice now and again, just the same.'

Marc received his plate with relish. 'Absolutely. Besides, better a dinner of herbs——' He stopped abruptly.

Joanna smiled brightly. 'Not quite in context, but I know what you mean. Now then, it's your turn. You've heard all about me. Talk about yourself for a change.'

Marc Anstey, plainly aware that she needed a change of subject, began to talk about the work he did in Washington for the *Sentinel*. Joanna listened, fascinated, as he opened a window for her into a world which sounded frenetic and glamorous to someone based in a quiet Oxfordshire village. Marc Anstey was in constant contact with people in the world of diplomacy, politics, business, with a sprinkling of the arts and entertainment industry as icing on the cake. Joanna was reluctantly impressed to hear that he spent a lot of time making use of a substantial expense account to wine and dine contacts, and travelled all over the United States to cover stories, as well as writing a weekly feature column for his newspaper.

'It all sounds a far cry from Swancote,' said Joanna wryly, as they sat over coffee at the kitchen table. 'Do you have a house or a flat of your own there?'

Marc shook his head. 'The perks of the job mean my own office, a car and a company apartment in return for my services.'

'You must be very well up in your profession!'

'Not as high as I intend to be, I assure you.' He smiled. 'I've been in the business a long time. In a couple of years I'll be forty. Sometimes I feel I've missed out on certain things in life.'

Joanna laughed. 'Not many, by what you've been saying.'

'I've never had a wife and family,' he said very quietly. 'Regular visits to see Rosa and Polly are the nearest thing I've ever managed in that direction.'

'No girlfriends?' Joanna couldn't help asking.

'Lady, I'm perfectly normal!' he retorted. 'Of course I've had girlfriends. I even considered a permanent relationship with one or two—but not for long.'

'Very wise,' said Joanna lightly. 'Saves a lot of wear and tear on the emotions, I assure you.'

'Some people have very successful, happy marriages,' he said, his eyes on the coffee he was stirring.

'I know. My best friend has one of those. Luck of the draw, I suppose—I got the short straw in mine.' Joanna jumped up to stack the tray, in sudden need of occupation.

'Since I couldn't pay for the meal, at least let me wash up,' said Marc.

'No need. The dishwasher Paul insisted on does that,' said Joanna cheerfully. 'I'll just load it up and we can go into the drawing-room—unless you mean to rush off straight away.'

'I don't,' said Marc emphatically, watching her as she moved about the kitchen. 'We haven't really touched on the points which need discussion.' He got up as she came towards him, looking at her in a way which flustered her a little. 'You know, don't you, that I find it hard to remember we met such a short time ago?'

Joanna's heart gave an errant thump as she led the way to the drawing-room, and she was thankful her face was hidden from him for a moment. By the time she'd curled up on the sofa and waved Marc to a chair she had herself well in hand again.

'It's only natural that you would feel like that,' she said reasonably. 'The circumstances which brought the meeting about were so traumatic it would be useless to pretend we're normal, polite acquaintances. Especially as Polly provides a constant reminder of—of the link between us.'

'You admit to a link, then?' he asked swiftly.

Joanna looked at him. 'I could hardly fail to, with Rosa and Paul to haunt us.'

He grimaced. 'Do you think one day you might bring yourself to think of me as just an ordinary guy? Not Rosa's brother or even Polly's uncle? Hell, Joanna, I possess an identity of my own, in case you hadn't noticed.'

Joanna smiled a little. 'Oh, I'd noticed.'

His eyes lit with an unsettling gleam. 'Good. Because although you bracket me with Rosa, there's no way I can think of you as Paul's wife.'

'Probably because for the past four years Paul couldn't, either——' Joanna stopped dead, turning her head away, furious to find herself close to tears. She sniffed hard, blinked violently, but it was no use. Suddenly the tears won, and she put her hands over her face in shame at her lack of self-control.

Marc crossed the room swiftly and took her in his arms, encouraging her as she sobbed without inhibition into his shirt front. She heard his voice, deep and husky as he murmured comfort, felt his hand on her hair, smoothing the heavy strands away from her forehead, and shut her eyes tightly as he put a fingertip under her chin to raise her face. She felt his lips brush her forehead, felt his arms tighten, then his mouth was hard and warm against hers and her quivering lips parted in surprise to the kiss which began as a caress meant to comfort, but metamorphosed into something different with alarming speed. In seconds Marc's arms were threatening to crack her ribs, and she was kissing him back, her tears drying on her burning cheeks.

Joanna pulled away, staring with drenched blue eyes into Marc's taut, astonished face as he reluctantly dropped his arms.

'I suppose I should say I'm sorry,' he muttered. 'Could I have a drink?'

'Yes.' Joanna cleared her throat. 'Yes, of course.'

'It won't affect my driving—just one finger of Scotch. I need it.' He got up without looking at her and went over to the tray of decanters Paul had insisted Joanna keep in readiness for visitors who rarely came to Swan House when he was there. 'Would you care for something?'

Joanna smoothed back her tumbled hair with an unsteady hand. 'Yes. Sherry, please. Dry.'

Marc handed her a glass, then went back to his chair, looking shaken. 'It was never my intention——'

'No, I realise that.' She downed half the sherry like medicine. 'I didn't mean to cry, either. I haven't much since—since Paul died.'

'It's no sin to cry.' He shrugged, staring down into his glass.

'Unless it's for the wrong reasons.'

He looked up sharply. 'What do you mean?'

Joanna looked bleak. 'What tears I've shed have been for myself, not Paul. At the funeral everyone thought I was grieving like a good widow should, and I felt sick inside at my own hypocrisy.'

'Stop it,' he said sharply. 'Paul was hardly the epitome of the normal, loving husband, was he? Why the hell should you grieve? Because it's the done thing in your particular social circles?'

'Don't talk rot,' she snapped, then glared at his sudden grin.

'That's better. Your eyes look beautiful when they smoulder. Much better than drowned in tears.'

Her eyes went on smouldering for a moment, then Joanna smiled reluctantly. 'I admit it's a relief to be able to explain to someone who knew—knew the truth. Of course I'm deeply sorry that Paul died in such a horrible way, but I just don't feel any great sense of personal loss. The real tragedy is that in the process of killing himself Paul had to kill Rosa too, and leave Polly motherless.'

'Is that why you agreed to take her?'

'No, not entirely.' Joanna hesitated. 'My reasons are less altruistic. I was shattered when I found I'd never have more babies after my accident. It may sound melodramatic, but taking on Polly fills a void nothing else can.' She jumped up restlessly. 'Enough soul-searching. Like some more coffee?'

Marc was tactful enough to go upstairs to check on Polly while she made it. By the time he rejoined Joanna in the drawing-room she was in full command of herself again and was able to greet Marc with a composed little smile, as though the kiss had never occurred.

'Polly all right?'

'Fine.' Marc looked at her searchingly. 'Are *you* all right, too?'

She nodded. 'Though why some people enjoy a good cry beats me. I feel like a wreck.'

He smiled. 'A very beautiful wreck.'

Joanna's lips twitched. 'Such tact!'

'Not at all. It's the truth.' He took a cup from her, his eyes meeting hers. 'Believe me, Joanna, I'm sorry I annoyed you last night. About the remarriage bit.'

She shrugged. 'When I'd calmed down a bit I could see your point.'

'How do you feel about marrying again?' he asked very quietly.

Joanna finished her coffee and replaced the cup on the tray with precision. 'To be honest, my experience of marriage, both my parents' and my own, has left me with a profound reluctance to repeat the experiment. Ever.'

'It could be different with another man.'

'Possibly. If I meet anyone likely to change my mind I'll let you know.'

Marc jumped up, unsmiling. 'Time I was off, I think.'

Joanna rose to her feet, dismayed to find that she quite badly wanted him to stay for a while. 'But there were things you needed to discuss.'

'I think we've covered everything.' He pulled on his jacket then paused in the hall. 'Give my love to Polly. May I come to see her when I get back? I don't know quite when it'll be.'

'Of course.' Joanna hesitated. 'Please believe that where access to Polly is concerned...' She halted, losing the thread of what she was saying as she met the look in his eyes. 'I—I mean you're welcome to come here as often as you want.'

'Am I?' He smiled sardonically. 'I know that's true where Polly's concerned. How about the lady of the house? Will I get a welcome from her, too?'

Joanna tore her eyes away from the hypnotic black gaze. 'Of course. Not quite as demonstrative, perhaps.'

'Why, Joanna?' Marc moved closer. 'Are you afraid of demonstrations of affection? Are you too much a coward to want to touch, to follow your natural, human instincts?'

Joanna backed away. 'No, of course not. I find it very easy to kiss and cuddle Polly.'

He followed her, backing her up against the newel post of the stairs, cutting off her retreat. 'For once I'm not concerned with Polly,' he said softly, his

voice so caressing that her knees began to knock
together. 'Won't you wish me *bon voyage* and speed
me on my way with a goodbye kiss, Joanna? Something I can remember when I'm far away?'

She swallowed. 'What happened just now was an
accident; you just meant to comfort me——'

'Right. Now I want a little comfort from you,
Joanna.'

'Oh, very well,' she said impatiently, and held
up her face. Marc laughed softly against her mouth
as his arms closed around her. Joanna, aghast at
her body's response to his nearness, clutched at his
jacket and he picked her up by the elbows and stood
her on the bottom stair so that her face was level
with his. The fire in his dark, explicit eyes took her
breath away, her lips parting in a gasp his mouth
stifled with a hard, demanding kiss which had little
to do with comfort. For a long, dizzying interval
Joanna gave herself up to an embrace so intimate
that she was left in no doubt that the man holding
her so close badly wanted a great deal more from
her than mere kisses. She burned with the knowledge that given the least encouragement he would
have carried her up to bed and abandoned all idea
of driving to London that night.

'You're kissing Jo!' said an accusing little voice.

Joanna pushed Marc away, heart pounding as
she smiled shakily at the small, pyjama-clad figure
at the head of the stairs. 'He was saying goodbye,
darling.'

'Not *he*,' said Polly impatiently. 'Marco!'

Marc bounded up the stairs to scoop his niece
up into his arms. 'What are you doing out of bed,

tesoro? When I came to see you just now you were fast asleep.'

'Want a drink,' said Polly, rubbing her eyes.

'Right,' said Joanna. She went ahead to the room which had once been hers, pulling herself together, giving herself a silent, stinging reproof for such abysmal behaviour. She handed Polly a drink, then watched as Marc tucked his niece up tenderly.

'See you when I get back, *cara*,' he said, kissing Polly's cheek. 'Be a good girl for Joanna.'

'Yes, Marco,' murmured Polly drowsily.

'Ciao, cara.'

Joanna bent to kiss the little girl, then followed Marc downstairs.

'Goodbye, then. Safe trip,' she said brightly, doing her level best to behave like any normal hostess seeing off a guest.

He smiled indulgently, then leaned down to kiss the tip of her nose. 'I hate goodbyes, Joanna Swan.' He strode to the door and opened it, then turned, lifting a hand in salute.

'My friends call me Jo,' she said on impulse.

Marc Anstey shook his black, curly head. 'Doesn't suit you—too masculine. You're all woman, whether you admit it or not. Besides, I'm not one of these *friends* of yours—my feelings for you have nothing to do with Plato! *Arrivederci*, Joanna.'

CHAPTER FIVE

THE period following Marc Anstey's departure for America proved one of the most harrowing, exhausting periods of Joanna's entire experience. Polly, coming to terms with a life from which the last familiar face had departed, relapsed into grief when she realised it would be some time before she saw her beloved Marco again. She threw tantrums, refused to eat, lost weight and generally worried Joanna to death.

'School started last week. Get them to take her this term instead of after Christmas,' advised Mary Lavenham one morning, while Polly was upstairs with Doris. 'I know she's a bit young, but it could be the answer, Jo.'

'She needs something,' said Joanna, sighing. 'She cries most nights for her mother, and in the day she pines for her uncle. As a mother substitute I'm a washout. I'm beginning to think I'm entirely the wrong person to have care of her.'

Mary pooh-poohed the idea. 'Nonsense. The poor little mite doesn't know how lucky she is, Jo.' She waved a hand about her expansively. 'A house like this, with that garden out there—think of the times we had here when we were children.'

Joanna sighed. 'I know. I just hope she settles down soon.'

'Get her to school,' repeated Mary, with the conviction of experience. 'I can't tell you what bliss it's been since Jack and Charlie started there last week.'

Joanna grinned. The Lavenham twins' recent brief visit to Swan House to play with Polly had been lively in the extreme. She could well believe Mary was delighted to have her sons safely occupied in school for a few hours each day. 'How a saint like George ever fathered a pair of devils like your twins I can't imagine!'

'He's not a saint *all* the time,' Mary said demurely. 'Must go. But take my advice, Jo. Send Polly to school right away. Has this uncle of hers been in touch?'

'Yes, of course. He talks to Polly each time, then she's back to square one again afterwards, worse than ever.'

'Then don't let him talk to her.' Mary pulled on an ancient quilted jerkin, eyeing Joanna closely. 'How are *you* coping, Jo? About Paul, I mean.'

Joanna shrugged. 'To be perfectly honest I don't have much time for brooding over Paul, owing to Polly.'

'Good,' said Mary, briskly, and patted Jo's cheek. 'Bring Polly to lunch on Saturday. George will be out marrying someone—and I'll bully the twins into submission, promise.'

Joanna took herself in hand when Mary was gone. Her friend's bracing comments had brought it home to her that she was too anxious to please where Polly was concerned. The child needed sympathy, it was true, but she also needed discipline and common sense if she was to make a complete recovery from the trauma of losing her mother.

While the child was still occupied Joanna rang the village school, had a chat with the deputy head teacher and arranged to take Polly there that very afternoon for a look round. It might, thought Joanna, have been better to consult Marc first. But Marc Anstey was caught up in the hectic whirl of life in Washington, not here on the spot, coping with Polly's tantrums, so she wouldn't bother.

Joanna was secretly very disappointed by his phone calls. To demonstrate how little their parting had affected her she'd been so crisp and cold when he'd first rung that he'd taken swift, easily discernible offence. Since then he'd kept rigidly to a single enquiry about Joanna's health before asking to speak to Polly, his hostile formality leaving Joanna thoroughly depressed. She'd been a fool to expect anything different, she assured herself. It was no big deal. She'd let Marc Anstey kiss her purely because she was in a particularly vulnerable state at the time. When he came to see Polly at Christmas she would make a point of clearing the air, letting him know that the incident was a one-off, never to be repeated.

Polly, to Joanna's relief, was not unwilling to visit the school. When she was ushered into a classroom full of busy, lively children painting in groups at small tables, she drank in the scene wide-eyed. The jolly, vivacious girl in charge seemed on excellent terms with her pupils, the Lavenham twins among them. Polly acknowledged their cheeky grins with a gracious nod, then walked home with Joanna afterwards, lost in thought.

'Would I paint too?'

'Of course, darling.'

'When can I go there?' demanded Polly.

'You can start on Monday, if you like.'

'When's Monday?'

'In four days' time.'

'Want to go tomorrow.'

'No, Polly. Mrs Phillips, the head teacher, said Monday.' Joanna waited, expecting a storm of protest, but Polly accepted it meekly enough. 'Let's go to the village shop and buy a drawing book and crayons, shall we?'

Marc rang that evening, not long after Polly was in bed, but this time Joanna went into the kitchen with the mobile phone and shut the door in case the child might hear.

'Would you mind if you didn't speak to Polly this time?' she asked, when the polite preliminaries were over.

'Why?' he demanded swiftly. 'Something wrong?'

'No. That's the point. There's nothing wrong at the moment, but if you talk to Polly there will be.' Joanna explained about the storms of weeping after his previous telephone conversations, and Marc swore softly, obviously very much taken aback.

'Hell, I'm sorry, Joanna. I didn't mean to complicate things. I thought it would reassure her to hear my voice.'

'So did I. Instead it makes her miss you all the more.' Joanna hesitated. 'Frankly, she seems to miss you even more than her mother—probably because she's accepted the fact that her mother's gone to heaven, whereas you're still available to her.'

'Does that mean you don't want me to visit her when I get back?' he demanded sharply.

'No. Of course not. But I don't think the telephone's a good idea. It unsettles her too much.' Joanna took a deep breath, then explained about the school, and how eager Polly was to start there.

'If she's been so difficult I imagine you're eager for her to start there too,' he said drily. 'She must be holding up your work.'

'I don't care about that!' said Joanna, stung. 'It's just that she's been grieving so much I thought she needed something to divert her, to occupy her mind. I've been frantic with worry about her.'

'I can see that.' He paused for a moment. 'May I make a suggestion?'

'Of course.'

'How about getting her a puppy? Didn't your ideal world include dogs before Paul Clifford put a stop to it?'

'I don't know why I haven't thought about that before,' she said, struck by the idea. 'Is Polly used to dogs?'

'No. But I'm sure she'll quickly *get* used to one if you feel up to coping with yet another call on your time.'

'Are you being sarcastic, Mr Anstey?'

'As it happens, no, *Mrs* Clifford. I'm not insensitive. I realise all this can't be easy for you. As far as I'm concerned you've got the go-ahead to do anything you want to make life easier, for both Polly and yourself.' He paused. 'Joanna?'

'Yes?'

'Since we seem to be communicating again, please don't hang up if I say I probably did myself a whole lot of no good where you're concerned before I left.'

Joanna stood very still, her knuckles white on the receiver. 'It was my fault for crying all over you.'

'I'm glad you did. Otherwise I'd have had no excuse for taking you in my arms. Which,' he added huskily, 'was where I wanted you from the moment I first set eyes on you, Paul Clifford's widow or not.'

Joanna almost dropped the telephone. She cleared her throat. 'I don't think you should be saying things like that to me.'

'I tried my best not to. Surely you've noticed how formal and correct I've been?' He chuckled, then the sound was drowned suddenly by a sudden high-pitched whine on the line, and after a few fruitless 'hellos' into the receiver Joanna replaced it on the handset. She sat down on a kitchen chair, staring into space for a long time before she went up to check on Polly, who, to her infinite relief, was asleep. Afterwards Joanna made herself some strong black coffee and focused her attention sternly on Marc Anstey's suggestion about a puppy for Polly, not sure if this was entirely a good idea. Puppies were small and lovable, but grew into big, unmanageable dogs if they weren't trained properly. Trying to get a little girl to see that she couldn't take a puppy to bed with her might be difficult. The answer was a fully grown dog in need of a home. Joanna rang Mary, her never-failing source on local information, who told her to get in touch with the local Labrador Rescue Group. Soon afterwards Joanna was able to explain her requirements to a sympathetic but brisk lady who asked to call round the following day to inspect the premises.

'You see, Mrs Clifford,' she explained, 'I must make it clear that we are looking for a home for a dog rather than finding a pet for you.'

Mrs Blake duly arrived the following day, took down particulars of Joanna's situation, noted Polly's age, and promised to match the splendidly suitable environs of Swan House with a dog in need of a home.

'Would you like a dog, Polly?' asked Joanna, when Mrs Blake had gone.

Polly was drawing on the kitchen table, as she usually was of late. She looked up, surprised. 'A dog?'

'Yes. We could take him for walks and play ball with him. He'd be great company.'

'That's a good idea, Polly,' said Doris. 'You'll like that.'

Doris's approval was more than enough to convince Polly a dog was a good idea on the whole. 'A big dog?' she asked doubtfully.

Joanna put out her hand at Labrador level. 'About so high. I used to have a dog,' she added casually.

'When you were a little girl like me?'

'Yes.'

'What was his name?'

'I had more than one, darling. When I was small we had one called Bunter, and then there was Pandora, and after that Mabel.'

Polly giggled. 'Funny names.' She went back to her drawing while Joanna made herself some coffee.

After a while she looked up. 'Jo, did you have a horse too, like Snowbird?'

'Yes,' said Joanna sadly. 'I did.' She brightened, astonished, as Polly pushed her sketch-book across the table. The child had made a very creditable attempt at a drawing of Snowbird, copied from one of Joanna's illustrations.

'But that's very good, Polly,' she said in wonder. 'What a clever girl you are. By the way, we're invited to the Rectory tomorrow, for lunch with Jack and Charlie.'

The child beamed. 'I'll wear my new trousers—and wellies.'

'Good choice, knowing the twins.'

That night, for the first time, Polly slept through without waking to cry for her mother. Joanna leapt out of bed early next morning in alarm, sure something was wrong, but she found Polly still fast asleep. Joanna stood very still in the doorway, just gazing at the child, realising just how deeply she'd been worried now those worries were allayed. Polly, she suddenly felt sure, was over the worst.

Lunch at the Rectory was a great success. So much so that George Lavenham returned from officiating at a wedding to find Joanna still chatting comfortably with his wife at the kitchen table, and Polly out in the garden with the twins, running about and shrieking happily at the top of her voice as they played some complicated form of tag.

George Lavenham was that paragon of the male species, a powerfully attractive man who was naturally virtuous, unshakeable in his faith, and, to Joanna's everlasting wonder, the possessor of a sense of humour.

He swept into the kitchen, looking like Joanna's idea of the Angel Gabriel with his fair hair gleaming like a beacon above his vestments. 'Joanna! You look better.'

'I feel better.' Joanna waved a hand towards the garden, where Polly was playing happily with George's sons. 'I think Polly's beginning to settle down at last.'

'She starts school on Monday,' said Mary, looking smug. 'I told Jo it was what she needed. I was right.'

'You're never wrong,' said her husband, kissing her. 'And even if you were it would take a braver man than me to point it out.'

Joanna watched them together, stabbed by a pang of envy. The Lavenhams gave out an aura of oneness her own marriage had never even approached. She got up quickly. 'I must go.'

'Must you, Joanna?' asked George, in tune, as always, with someone else's pain. 'Why not stay for supper? I'm sure Mary can peel another potato or whatever. I can run you home afterwards.'

'Super idea,' said Mary warmly. 'Do stay, Jo.'

Dangerously tempted, Joanna nevertheless found the strength from somewhere to refuse. 'Thanks a lot. But we must go home.' She smiled. 'Best to leave while Polly's enjoying herself. She gets fractious when she's tired.'

'Don't we all?' sighed George, accepting a cup of coffee. He gave Joanna an affectionate smile. 'Next time, then.'

Marc rang again that night. Before he had time to say a word Joanna embarked on a bright, impersonal account of the pleasant day at the Rectory, told him about Polly's drawing and gave him her views on the advisability of a fully grown dog instead of a puppy.

Marc listened patiently until she finished, then chuckled. 'All right, Joanna. I get the message. I'll leave more personal exchanges until we meet again. Face to face,' he added significantly. 'But where Polly's concerned do whatever you like to make life easier. I know you'll do what's best for her. If I hadn't believed that I'd never have left her with you, no matter what Rosa said.'

'Perhaps a fully trained nanny might have done better with her than I have,' said Joanna, sighing.

'Rot! She needs love, not efficiency.' He paused. 'I believe you possess a great deal of love to give, Joanna.'

Something in the way his voice roughened on the last words took Joanna's breath away.

'Polly's easy to love,' she said unevenly.

'So am I!'

'It's not you we're discussing!' Joanna hesitated. 'By the way, Polly keeps asking when you're coming home again.'

'I'm working on it. Just tell her soon, will you? As soon as I possibly can. I miss you. Both of you.'

Joanna caught sight of her face in the hall mirror as she replaced the phone; eyes like stars and a flush which deepened as she realised that Polly wasn't alone in wanting to know when Marc was coming home. It was useless to tell herself that Paul had been dead only a short time, that a respectable widow shouldn't be thinking of another man at all at this stage. The truth of the matter was simple. It was such a long, long time since she'd felt like a

wife that it was impossible to think of herself as a
widow. Nor, she told herself firmly, was it a crime
to find herself strongly drawn to Marc Anstey. He
was an attractive, intelligent man who made it clear
he found her desirable, an attitude which poured
balm on the wounds made by Paul's infidelity.

She sighed. On the other hand, it was a bad idea
to throw herself into Marc's arms at the drop of a
hat however much she wanted to. Because of Polly
the only relationship possible between them was
friendship. A love affair, deeply tempting prospect
though it might be, was out of the question.

Polly took to school like a duck to water, even
happy to have her lunch there once she found Jack
and Charlie Lavenham ate theirs in school too.

'You won't know you're born, Mrs Clifford,' said
Doris the first day.

Joanna, who felt illogically restless now she had
several hours all to herself, smiled ruefully. 'I felt
terrible when I handed her over this morning, Doris.
I don't know why! Polly went skipping off with the
Lavenham twins without a qualm.'

For a while that first day Joanna pottered about,
finding things to do instead of shutting herself in
the study. But at last, mindful of recent hints from
her editor, she sat down at her desk and began,
very slowly at first, but eventually with her usual
concentration, to work on the Snowbird adventure
abandoned when Polly arrived to disrupt her life.

Once the new routine was established, the days
began to fly by. Polly, stimulated and diverted by
her lessons and the company of other children, was
a very different little person. There were times when

she still lapsed into grief for her mother, or anxiety over seeing Marc again, but with the resilience of childhood she gradually began to accept her new way of life, an acceptance which speeded up enormously once Sunny arrived on the scene.

Sunny was a golden Labrador, two years old, whose owners had been posted to a job abroad and couldn't take him along.

'His neutered and well-trained,' said Mrs Blake on the telephone. 'A very attractive dog, and used to children, Mrs Clifford. His owners are heartbroken at having to part with him. Would you care to come and see him?'

Two hours later, Joanna, who fell madly in love with Sunny at first sight, had the dog on a lead as she waited outside the school. When Polly ran out with the Lavenham twins, she stopped dead as she saw Joanna with a dog.

'Is that ours?' she demanded, scarlet-faced with excitement.

Rejoicing at the word 'ours', Joanna nodded casually. 'Do you like him?'

'Go on, pat him,' exhorted Jack Lavenham, and Polly, gingerly at first, then more boldly, stroked Sunny's handsome head. The dog, panting gently, looking as though he were grinning from ear to ear, submitted to the caress with such obvious pleasure that Joanna soon had to restrain all three children from giving the dog concussion with their attentions.

'Good move, that dog,' approved Mary. 'Now let me get my little darlings off the poor beast before the RSPCA come down on us.'

Sunny was a very well-trained, beautifully be-haved dog, and no trouble at all from the first. It was Polly who posed the problems encountered in the first few days of dog-ownership. She yearned to feed him titbits from the table, and protested stormily because Joanna said Sunny couldn't go upstairs.

'He's a dog, Polly,' said Joanna firmly. 'He'll be much happier if we keep to the rules. And healthier,' she added, 'if you don't keep giving him bits and pieces to eat. He'll grow fat. And if he's fat he'll be ill.'

Polly, quick to learn, thought this over and de-cided she hated the idea of Sunny being ill, and kept meticulously to Joanna's instructions from then on.

'She adores him,' reported Joanna when Marc rang towards the end of the week. 'She hasn't cried for Rosa at all since Sunny arrived.'

'My idea was a good one, then,' said Marc smugly.

Joanna chuckled. 'An absolute brainwave!'

'If Polly's still asking when I'm coming home, by the way,' he went on casually, 'I am.'

'You're what?'

'Home. I'm in London. I arrived today, jet-lagged, death warmed up, but home.'

Joanna sat down abruptly. 'Oh. I didn't re-alise——'

'I bade a fond farewell to Washington yesterday, I caught a flight today—or is it tomorrow?' He waited for a while. 'Are you still there, Joanna?'

'Yes. I'm here.' Joanna gathered her dazed wits together hurriedly. 'Shall I tell Polly you'll see her soon?'

'I'll be tied up at the paper until Saturday. If I drive down to Swancote on Sunday morning, could I take you both out to lunch?'

'I'll cook lunch,' said Joanna quickly. 'If you like, that is.'

'I like very much. See you Sunday.'

When Polly heard her uncle was coming to lunch at the weekend her eyes were like stars.

'He can come when we take Sunny for a walk. He'll like Sunny, won't he? Can I get down, please?' Barely waiting for Joanna's permission she left the breakfast table to crouch down by the dog, telling him how much he'd like Marco, and what fun it would be to go for walks together.

Joanna watched indulgently, wondering how Marc would react to the change in his niece. Polly was a different child from the woebegone little creature he'd left behind.

Instead of racing by, time dragged interminably until the weekend. In vain Joanna ordered herself to stop behaving like a schoolgirl with her first crush. She had to force herself to concentrate on her work, to banish the clever, olive-skinned face which kept coming between her eyes and the page. She was glad when Friday afternoon came round at last, and she could officially abandon work for the weekend.

'What's up?' demanded Mary, as they waited outside the school for their charges. 'You're like a cat on hot bricks. Work going badly?'

'Concentration's bad,' said Joanna with truth.

'Hardly surprising, is it!' Mary eyed her, frowning. 'Something wrong, Jo?'

Joanna smiled sheepishly. 'Nothing more than usual. Life's a bit hectic these days, that's all. Not that I'm complaining,' she added hastily.

'You're not brooding over Paul?'

'Paul?' Joanna turned wide blue eyes on her friend.

'Yes, Paul,' said Mary drily. 'Your husband.'

Joanna blushed to the roots of her hair. 'No. Oh, Mary, I should be. But I'm not.'

'Glad to hear it,' said Mary succinctly, then waved. 'Brace yourselves. Here they come.'

Happily Saturday was a fine, sunny day which meant Joanna could channel both her own and Polly's energies by taking Sunny on walks as long as Polly's small legs would allow. Jack and Charlie came to tea, which put the finishing touch to both her own and Polly's exhaustion, and once George had collected the twins and Polly was in bed Joanna retreated to put her feet up on the sofa with a new novel. Sunny, apparently as glad as Joanna for a rest, lay stretched out on the floor beside her, snoring gently, while Joanna planned her menu for the next day. She smiled dreamily, abandoning any attempt to disguise the fact that she was as excited as Polly over seeing Marc Anstey again.

After the large doses of fresh air Joanna felt drowsy in the warmth of the drawing-room. Her eyes grew heavy and the book slid, unnoticed, to the floor as she dozed. Suddenly she woke with a start, to see Marc's face, disembodied at the window. For a moment she thought she was dreaming, that his face was some kind of wish fulfilment, then she realised he was smiling and disturbingly real, and she felt a great rush of joy at the sight of him. Stealthily, in an effort to leave the dog sleeping undisturbed, she tiptoed on bare feet from the drawing-room and closed the door behind her before racing across the hall to fling open the door.

'I'm a little early for Sunday lunch,' said Marc without preamble and seized her in his arms, kissing her fiercely, in a famished, unstoppable way which left Joanna unsteady on her feet when he released her.

'I've been dreaming of that,' he said huskily.

'I wasn't expecting you until tomorrow,' said Joanna breathlessly. She brushed past him to close the door with hands which shook so much that she could hardly shoot the bolt.

'I managed to finish up earlier than I thought, so instead of going back to my lonely flat I rang the Lamb and Flag in Swancote, bespoke me a room for the night, then drove down here like a bat out of hell.' He reached out a hand to touch her cheek. 'Are you glad to see me?'

'Would there be any point in denying it?' she asked mockingly.

His eyes danced. 'No. Not after that kiss.' He looked about him. 'Where's this guard-dog of yours, by the way?'

'Asleep in the drawing-room.' Joanna opened the door. 'Here, Sunny. Here, boy. Come and say hello.'

Sunny was shameless in his predilection for the new arrival. Joanna chuckled as the dog fawned over Marc. 'He obviously fancies you like mad.'

'Never mind the dog—does his owner feel the same? If not madly, at least a little.'

He turned to look at her so suddenly that Joanna had to think fast. 'Even if I do, I'm not going to let myself,' she blurted.

His eyes narrowed. 'Am I allowed to ask why?'

'Because I'm too vulnerable at the moment. You must be, too, in a different kind of way.' Joanna's chin went up. 'If ever—I mean if we were to become involved in that way I'd want it to be for normal, healthy reasons, not because our link with Rosa pushed us together.'

'Shall I go out and come in again then?' he asked with sarcasm. 'I find it a little difficult to revert to formality now, after that kiss.'

She grinned. 'I don't require formality, Mr Anstey. Let's just be friends. Good friends, of course.'

'With the accent on the "good".' His eyes lingered deliberately on her mouth. 'It seems a pity. Would you believe that while I was in the States I resisted quite a few blandishments just because of your beautiful blue eyes?'

'I'll try,' said Joanna tartly, leading the way into the kitchen. 'Shall I make you something to eat now?'

'No. I had a large celebratory lunch. I'd like some coffee, though, and while you make it will Sunny here let me go up to see Polly?'

'Try him.'

Sunny was quite happy to let Marc upstairs. He made it plain he would have liked to go too, but in response to Marc's command the dog lay obediently at the foot of the stairs, waiting with his handsome head raised in longing for this new, fascinating human to return.

'Polly looks well!' said Marc, coming into the kitchen. He closed the door behind him. 'She's sleeping like a log.'

'Now we have Sunny we walk a lot. The fresh air knocks her out.' Joanna poured coffee for them both, then sat down at the kitchen table. 'So how was Washington?'

'Hectic.' Marc sat down opposite her, looking to Joanna's eyes even more attractive than before now some of the lines of grief were smoothed from his lean, dark face. He smiled into her eyes, reaching a hand across the table to touch hers. 'How have you been, Joanna?'

'At first it was hard going,' she admitted, withdrawing her hand gently. 'After you'd gone Polly relapsed badly, as I told you. But since she started school she's been a different child.' Joanna explained about the help the Lavenhams had given, and how Polly liked playing with the twins. 'Then Sunny came on the scene.' Joanna grinned. 'She's been telling him how much he's going to like you, and she was right!'

'Children and dogs always like me,' said Marc smugly, eyes gleaming. 'It's a good indication of a chap's character. Paul hated dogs, which proves my point.'

There was a sudden, charged silence, then Marc shook his head. 'Sorry, Joanna.'

She shrugged. 'You can't help how you feel, I suppose. And we can't pretend Paul never existed. He did. And until recently, too. I keep feeling that a widow with any pretensions to sensitivity wouldn't even be here with you like this. We hardly know each other, really, Marc.'

'Owning to pressures beyond our control we've got to know each other faster and more intimately than we'd ever have done if we'd met in the usual way.' He captured her hand again, caressing it gently. 'Nothing on earth will alter the fact that Rosa and Paul are gone. But you and I are here and alive, Joanna. Is it so terrible to be attracted to each other? Neither of us is hurting someone else, as Paul and Rosa did. Paul was no husband to you, not for years, anyway. Why should you feel guilty about wanting to live and——?' He stopped short, his eyes completing the sentence for him as they held hers.

'I see your point,' she admitted. 'But I doubt if the world at large would feel the same.'

'I don't give a damn about the world at large. The opinion I care about is yours.'

'Is it? Then in my considered opinion we should go into reverse a little. Get to know each other better before——' She paused, flushing.

'You stopped at the interesting bit.'

'You know perfectly well what I mean.'

Marc smiled. 'Yes, Joanna. I know exactly what you mean. And I won't tease you any more. I'll do my utmost to behave. But it won't be easy,' he added, his caressing eyes bringing heat to her cheeks.

They spent the rest of the evening in the drawing-room, Sunny on the floor beside Marc's chair while they caught up with each other's news.

'You must be pretty tired,' she commented, after yawns began to punctuate Marc's conversation rather regularly.

'I haven't caught up on myself yet. I've been working flat out to get back home to finalise a little matter I embarked on some time ago.' He stretched luxuriously, looking very pleased with himself.

'Am I allowed to ask what it is?' asked Joanna, curiously.

'A new job. It was confirmed today. As from the first of next month I shall no longer go a-roving to foreign parts. I shall be foreign editor of the *Citadel*, and based in London. Are you going to congratulate me?'

Joanna looked at him uncertainly. 'I don't know yet. How will the new arrangement affect Polly—and me?'

Marc stared at her, astonished. 'You don't honestly think I'd take her away from you now that she's settling down in Swancote?' He paused. 'Unless that's what you want, of course.'

'Of course it isn't,' she snapped. 'How can you even suggest such a thing?'

He passed a hand over his face, then leaned forward in his chair. 'Shall I tell you why I put in for the new job, Joanna Swan? Because it meant being based permanently in the UK. And why did I want that? So I could see more of you—and Polly too, of course. It beats me how you could think I'd take her away from you!'

Joanna quailed before the fierce light in his eyes. 'I'm sorry, I'm sorry.' She pushed a glossy wing of hair back from her face. 'It's just that I've grown so attached to her already—I couldn't bear the thought of losing her.'

His eyes softened. 'I realise that. So, now you've had time to calm down, am I allowed to ask if you welcome the idea of having me around more often? In my function as Polly's legal guardian, of course.'

'I think I can handle that,' said Joanna matter-of-factly, hoping he had no inkling of how much the idea thrilled her. 'Were there many people after the job?'

'Hundreds! But with me in the running, of course, no one else stood a chance.'

'So modest!'

He gazed at her, sighing. 'This is going to be very difficult for me, Joanna.'

'What is?'

'Trying to keep my distance. You must know I'm straining every muscle to stay where I am instead of coming over there and taking you in my arms.'

'Take Sunny for a walk in the garden instead,' she said briskly. 'I'll make some sandwiches while you're out.'

Marc laughed ruefully and jumped to his feet, clicking his fingers to the willing dog. 'You're a cruel lady. Come on, hound. Let's go cool off in the night air.'

Joanna felt absurdly happy as she put a snack together in the kitchen. It was useless to tell herself that a woman who was thirty next birthday shouldn't be feeling like a starry-eyed teenager, that one look from Marc Anstey's black eyes shouldn't be enough to melt all her resistance. Not that she was going to let him know that it did. Nor, she thought bleakly, was she going to let him make love to her, no matter how much she wanted him to. It was all too sudden, too new. They had known each other far too short a time to rush into something which would inevitably end in tears. Polly's, as well as her own.

CHAPTER SIX

JOANNA woke next morning to a feeling of anticipation she knew at once was due to Marc's unexpected reappearance. She sang off-key as she showered and dressed, deciding to stop worrying about relationships and just enjoy the day with a fascinating, charismatic man who made it flatteringly clear he found her desirable. She put on a new strawberry-pink wool shirt and grey flannel trousers then went in to Polly, who was sitting up in bed, tongue between her teeth in intense concentration as she sketched the row of battered teddies on the shelf. Polly held up her face to be kissed, then went on with her masterpiece while Joanna marvelled at the way the child had contrived, with a minimum of basic lines, to portray the characteristics of each separate bear.

'Goodness, darling,' said Joanna. 'That *is* good.'

'I like drawing.'

'I know you do. But could you go back to it later? Sunny needs a walk.'

Polly agreed.

'Guess who came to see us last night?' said Joanna, smiling, when they were out in the garden.

Polly's bright black eyes looked puzzled. 'I don't know. Who, Jo?'

'Your uncle! He came home a day early.'

Polly stared, her lower lip quivering. 'Marco! Didn't he come to see me?'

'Of course he did, the moment he arrived. But you were fast asleep. Don't look like that,' added Joanna hastily, bending to hug the child. 'He's staying in the village. He'll be here soon.'

In wild excitement the child went careering round in circles with the barking dog, too pent-up at the thought of seeing her beloved Marco again to eat much breakfast when they went in. Joanna hadn't the heart to scold her. She couldn't eat much herself. And *she* was old enough to know better, she reminded herself as she began preparations for the celebration lunch.

The reunion between Marc Anstey and Polly was touching to see, the presence of an excited, barking Sunny a welcome touch of lightness as the child wept with joy to see her uncle again.

'Hey,' said Marc huskily, 'you mustn't cry, *tesoro*! Look, you're upsetting Sunny!'

Quick to comfort the dog, Polly forgot her tears as she pulled Marc into the house and began to talk nineteen to the dozen about the Lavenham twins, and all the new friends she'd made, and the lessons she did at school.

'I like drawing the best,' she told Marc happily.

'I know. A little bird told me.' Marc smiled at Joanna, who was standing a little way apart to allow the other two their moment of reunion. 'And how are you this morning, Joanna?'

'I'm just fine, thank you,' she said with composure. 'Let's go into the kitchen so I can keep an eye on lunch.'

Marc winked at Polly. 'You two go ahead. I've got one or two things to get out of the car.'

'What things?' demanded Polly.

'Wait and see—off you go with Joanna, please.'

By the time Marc finally joined them in the kitchen, weighed down by a large parcel, Polly was jumping up and down with excitement, chattering like a magpie as she hazarded guesses about the contents.

Joanna helped her with the string and brown paper while Marc sat back in a kitchen chair, watching the two intent faces, the one rosy beneath a mop of curls, the other creamy pale under a shining wing of dark gold hair. Joanna's eyes narrowed as she glanced up to intercept the dark, intent look trained on her face.

'A lot of paper!' she commented.

'Just tear it off,' he advised, 'before Polly goes off with a loud report!'

Soon the last of the wrappings were off, discarded on the floor for Sunny to investigate, while Polly gazed, saucer-eyed, at a drawing-board and easel, each a miniature of Joanna's. With them came a package of white cartridge paper, drawing books, a box of paints, one full of coloured pencils, another with felt-tip pens, everything a child could possibly need to paint and draw and colour to her heart's content.

'Well?' demanded Marc. 'Do you like your surprise?'

For answer Polly hurled herself into his arms and covered his face with smacking kisses to express her delight.

'Did you bring a present for Jo?' she demanded at last.

'Of course I did. I left it out in the hall. Fetch the parcel on the hall table, *cara*—and carry it very, very carefully, please.'

Joanna eyed him disapprovingly as she gathered up discarded wrappings. 'You needn't have brought me anything.'

'Why not?' His eyes locked with hers. 'It seemed the natural thing to do. I thought of you a lot while I was away. Did you ever spare a thought for me?'

'You promised——' She broke off, jumping up as Polly came back into the room with Sunny at her heels. She handed a package to Joanna in great excitement.

'Go on, Jo,' she urged. 'Open it.'

Wishing she could have done so away from two pairs of identical black eyes, Joanna unwrapped her gift with unusual clumsiness, lifting the lid of a cardboard box at last to find a mass of polystyrene chips, and at the heart of them a tissue-swathed object which she unwrapped with care then stood still, her teeth caught in her bottom lip. The pearl-white porcelain horse in her hands was depicted in full gallop, mane and tail flying, the workmanship so exquisite that she blenched at the thought of what it must have cost.

'It's Snowbird!' cried Polly in wonder.

Joanna stood the horse gently on the kitchen table. 'No, darling. Snowbird's a pony. This is a horse, like my Saladin. The very image of him, in fact.' She looked at Marc. 'How did you know? That he looked just like this?'

'I didn't. But I hoped. I came across it by chance in Kensington only a couple of days ago.' He smiled. 'The moment I saw it I thought of you.'

'Aren't you going to kiss Marc to say thank you?' asked Polly severely.

Joanna, eyes averted, planted a very swift kiss on Marc's lean dark cheek. 'Now,' she said briskly. 'Where shall we put him?'

Marc consulted Polly earnestly. 'I think he should sit on the desk in the study, don't you? Perhaps he'll give Joanna inspiration.'

Joanna nodded. 'Yes. You're right. I shall want him where I can see him all the time.' And where no one else was likely to see the horse at all, or ask embarrassing questions about where she'd acquired it.

To Joanna the day was a bittersweet blend of pleasure and misgiving, the latter increasing with every minute as the three of them spent the day in much the same way that countless other families were spending a fine autumn Sunday all over the country. They ate a traditional roast lunch together, then went for a walk through the woods with Sunny until it was time for tea, and to the casual eye they appeared like any mother, father and child. But, Joanna took care to remind herself, they were not. Polly was in her care, but the child was not her daughter, nor was Marc Anstey anything other than Polly's uncle. And days together like this could be misleading for Polly, if she got into the habit of regarding the three of them as a family unit.

'Penny for your thoughts,' said Marc lazily, as he stroked the dog's head.

Joanna took refuge in gathering up plates and cups. 'Not for sale,' she said lightly.

'Perhaps I knew what you were thinking,' he said so softly that Polly, absorbed in drawing Sunny, couldn't hear.

'I doubt it.' Joanna hefted the tray, refusing his help. 'What time do you have to leave?'

'Once Polly's in bed I'd better make tracks. Busy day tomorrow.'

Joanna nodded, deeply relieved, yet illogically disappointed at the same time. 'While I see to this lot perhaps you'd like to chivvy Polly into the bath.'

'Right.' Marc got to his feet, yawning. 'Come on, *cara*. Bathtime.'

All too soon, it seemed to Joanna, Polly was in bed and asleep, and Marc was ready to go.

'I don't have to go,' he said, eyeing her narrowly as she walked with him to the door. 'Given the least encouragement I'd stay. For a while at least. But you're on edge, Joanna. And I wish I knew why. Last night I surprised you into giving me a totally spontaneous welcome. But today you're back in your shell and regretting your lapse last night, yet too polite to tell me to get lost. What's troubling you, Joanna? Tell me.'

Joanna faced him. 'All right,' she said flatly. 'If you must know, I'm worried because the type of day we spent together is certain to be bad for Polly.'

His eyes narrowed incredulously. 'How the hell do you work that out?

'Surely you can see! Polly will take it for granted it's the way things are always going to be.' Joanna eyed him unhappily. 'And you and I know perfectly well we can't guarantee that.' She put out a hand in appeal. 'Please don't be angry. It's been a lovely day. I've enjoyed it as much as Polly. But circumstances rule out any kind of—of attachment between you and me, Marc. You've got to make it clear to Polly that one day you'll probably produce some perfectly acceptable aunt for her. Just as I may find another husband.'

'Is this an oblique way of telling me you already have?' he said harshly.

She shook her head, hugging her arms across her chest. 'No. I'm not. If I had I wouldn't——'

'Wouldn't have let me kiss you senseless last night!' Black eyes met incensed blue ones challengingly. 'Well?' he went on. 'Isn't that what happened?

'No,' she said hotly. 'I was too taken by surprise to—to resist, that's all. It didn't mean anything other than that.'

'My mistake. I thought it meant a hell of a lot more than that.' He took her by the shoulders, his fingers digging into her skin through her sweater. 'I could have sworn that I got through to the real you, that you were so glad to see me you forgot that you were Paul Clifford's widow, and I was Rosa's brother. For a moment there we were just two people who'd missed each other and were so bloody delighted to be together again that what happened was the most natural thing in the world.'

'But that's what I'm worried about,' she cried, trying to free herself. 'Can't you see, Marc? I acknowledge the chemistry between us. It's—it's undeniable. But that kind of thing can vanish and leave nothing behind in a relationship. And today we looked like a family, we behaved like a family; a permanent arrangement, which we're not. We're two strangers thrown together by chance, with Polly as the sole point of reference between us other than the chemistry.'

'Is that really what you think?' he said in disbelief. He stood back, his arms falling to his sides. 'You think that without Polly I wouldn't have driven down here like a love-sick schoolboy last night. That I wouldn't have bought you the horse——'

'Which you shouldn't have done—it must have cost a fortune.'

He gave her a look like a thrown spear. 'Bloody fool, wasn't I? But when I found it, all I could see was the look in those big blue eyes when you talked about your beloved Saladin.'

Joanna's head went up angrily. 'I'd rather you hadn't given it to me, whatever your reason. Look, Marc, it's better to put the brakes on now, not when it's too late. The very nature of our link with Polly is bound to have a greenhouse effect on our relationship if we're not careful, forcing it into something intimate whether we want it or not.'

He stood with folded arms, his face grim. 'And you don't, obviously. All right, Joanna. What do you suggest? That I don't come down here any more?'

'Of course not,' she said impatiently. 'Polly needs to see you. I know that.' Her eyes fell before the ice in his. 'But I suggest that next time you take Polly out on your own. I'll make sure she knows well in advance that I'm not available that day. She'll probably be delighted to have you all to herself.'

'Am I allowed to pick her up at the house?' asked Marc bitingly.

'Of course. Please! Don't make this more difficult than it is.' She looked at him in entreaty. 'I've had time to think—last night after you'd gone, today while we were out walking. I know I'm right. Polly must get used to the fact that, while you and I are both constants in her life, we are totally separate from each other.'

Marc gave a short, mirthless laugh. 'I'm sorry for you, Joanna. I don't know what—or who—made you so wary of human relationships, though I can make a bloody good guess. We could be good together. I'm as certain of that as night follows day. Tell me. How long is a guy required to know you before——?'

'Before what?' she broke in hotly. 'Before I let him into my bed?'

'I was going to say before you considered him worthy of trust, Joanna.' He turned away, suddenly, repudiation in every line of his lean, graceful body. 'Oh, what the hell! I don't know why I'm beating my head against a stone wall like this. All right. You win. We'll play the game to your rules if that's the way you want it. I just hope Polly understands.'

Joanna, aware that she should be satisfied now she had her way, felt instead as though all the warmth had just drained out of her life.

'Will you come again next week?' she forced herself to ask.

'Yes. I'll come,' he said morosely. 'I'll be round about eleven next Sunday to take Polly out to lunch. I leave it to you to explain why you're not honouring us with your presence. Goodnight, Mrs Clifford.' Marc opened the door without a backward glance, as though he couldn't bear to look at her, closing the heavy oak door behind him so quietly that the effect was worse than if he'd slammed it in her face.

When the following weekend arrived there was no need to fabricate an excuse for reneging on Polly's outing with Marc. Joanna had the messiest, most objectionable head cold she'd ever had in her life, and felt, looked and sounded so wretched that Mary Lavenham insisted Polly spend Saturday at the Rectory, and remain there overnight, away from Joanna's germs.

'You're a saint,' said Joanna hoarsely from the top of the stairs, as the small cortège prepared to depart, dog included.

'Wrong Lavenham. Sanctity is George's department.' Mary shooed Polly out of the door then looked up at Joanna, lips pursed. 'You're a mess. Get back in bed, so you're fit to have Polly back in the morning. Sorry I can't keep her tomorrow, too, but you know what Sundays are like *chez* Lavenham.'

'I do. In any case, tomorrow she's off on a jaunt with her uncle.'

'Hmm. I'd like to meet this uncle of Polly's some time. He can't possibly be as amazing as she says.'

Joanna made non-committal noises, thanked Mary gratefully, then went to wave to Polly from the window before going back to bed in utter misery, coughing, barely able to breathe, sneezing at such regular intervals that the tip of her nose soon shone red like a traffic light from contact with too many paper tissues.

When the telephone rang late in the afternoon Joanna felt almost too wretched to answer it. Only the thought that it might be Mary with an emergency gave her the necessary energy to lift the receiver.

'Hello?' she said thickly, then gave way to a bout of coughing.

'Joanna?' demanded Marc. 'What the hell's the matter?'

'Got a cold.'

'Only a cold? You sound at death's door. Where's Polly?'

'At the Rectory.' Joanna sneezed three times in rapid succession. 'They're keeping her overnight,' she gasped when she could speak. 'I should be better tomorrow.'

'You can hardly be much worse by the sound of you! Did Polly mind?' he added.

'Mind?'

'Sleeping somewhere else.'

'No. She seemed quite keed—keen. She took Sunny with her. She'll be ready when you come tomorrow. You *are* coming, I suppose?' she asked anxiously, shuddering at the thought of Polly's disappointment if he wasn't.

'Yes. See you in the morning, then.'

Joanna sagged against the pillows in relief. 'Right. Goodbye.'

'For Pete's sake take something for that cold,' he ordered. *'Ciao.'*

Joanna spent a miserable night feeling sorry for herself, her misery somewhat alleviated when she staggered downstairs the following morning to find

Doris on the doorstep with Polly, Sunny and various bags and baggage.

'Good morning,' Doris said calmly, smiling at Joanna's astonishment. 'You do look poorly, and that's a fact. No, Polly, you mustn't hug Mrs Clifford, you'll get her cold.'

'All right,' said Polly reluctantly, her eyes anxious on Joanna's ashen face and red, puffy eyes. 'Are you very ill, Jo?'

'No, not really, darling,' said Joanna, pulling herself together as she stood back for them to come in. 'I feel horrible, and a bit shivery, but only the way you do with a cold. And don't think I'm not grateful for your presence, Doris,' she added, 'but how——?'

'Mrs Lavenham rang me last night. She was worried about you,' said Doris, removing her best coat with care. 'I know what Sundays are like at the Rectory, so I said I'd see to you. I've packed my two off for the day to get spoiled by their Gran.'

Within minutes of Doris's arrival Joanna was back in a bed newly made up with clean linen, a tray of steaming coffee and crisp toast beside her and a hot water bottle at her feet. Polly, allowed to stand in the open doorway for a chat, gazed at her with round, apprehensive eyes.

'Jo. . . do colds ever make people die?'

Joanna's heart contracted. She summoned up a reassuring smile as she said firmly, 'No, Polly. Never, ever. I'll be up and about again by this afternoon. I'm only staying here now so I don't give you my germs. Now while I eat the delicious breakfast tell me what you did yesterday at the Lavenhams'.'

Her eyes bright with relief, Polly lingered a while to give an account of her stay with the twins, displayed a bruise she'd gained by sliding down the Rectory banisters, then decided she'd better play ball with Sunny in the garden for a while before getting ready to go out with Marco. She lingered for a moment to discuss her choice of outfit for the outing, then went off downstairs to Doris, plainly no longer a prey to fears about Joanna's mortality.

Marc Anstey arrived a little after eleven. When Doris let him in the sound of his deep voice carried to Joanna's room, but not loudly enough to let her know what he was saying. Shortly afterwards Polly peered cautiously round the door. She displayed herself to Joanna in all the glory of a new scarlet sweater and navy trousers, announced she was ready to go, then blew a kiss and ran off to join Marc.

'I told Mr Anstey you weren't well enough for a visit,' said Doris firmly when all was quiet. She plumped up Joanna's pillows then handed her some freshly squeezed orange juice and a couple of cold-cure tablets.

'Thank you, Doris,' said Joanna meekly. 'But don't hang about here too long, or you'll catch my cold.'

'I never get colds. Malcolm and Sheila won't be back until the eight o'clock bus, so I'll stay until Polly's bedtime, Mrs Clifford.'

'I feel guilty lying here,' sighed Joanna. 'It's only a cold, Doris.'

'But a very nasty one.' Doris hesitated at the door, looking a little awkward. 'Your resistance is low, I expect.'

Lower than Doris imagined, thought Joanna,
once she was alone. And to more dangerous things
than the common cold. In a day or two her coughs
and sneezes would be better, but where Marc Anstey
was concerned she had a sinking feeling that recovery would take longer. Like the rest of her life,
perhaps.

Joanna sighed. It was useless to pretend that she
was indifferent to Marc. His slightest touch set off
fireworks of response inside her that she'd never
felt for Paul. But she just couldn't conquer her deep
distrust of the sudden longing to give herself up to
a man, body and soul. It would be bliss with Marc
while it lasted, she knew, a shiver running through
her at the mere thought. But when it ended, as experience had taught her it could, Polly would be
heartbroken. And the mere thought of causing the
child more grief again was unendurable.

When Marc returned with Polly later in the
afternoon Doris was still firmly in charge. She offered Marc a cup of tea, which he refused, gave
him the latest bulletin on Joanna's health, took
charge of the flowers he'd brought for the invalid,
then saw him calmly to the door with Polly, who
waved him off, blowing kisses, then scampered up
to Joanna.

'Marco didn't stay,' she told Joanna from the
doorway. 'Are you better, Jo?'

'Yes, darling. Have you had a lovely time?'

Polly was surprisingly non-committal. Marco had
taken her to lunch and then for a drive, during
which they'd stopped to go for a walk, but they'd
had to run back to the car because it rained. 'You

come next time,' said Polly firmly. 'We missed you, Jo.'

'I thought you'd prefer being on your own together,' said Joanna surprised.

Polly shook her head. 'No. I like it best when you come, too.'

'I think Doris has made some kind of little cakes for you,' said Joanna, guiltily pleased that she'd been missed.

'Yum,' said Polly eagerly, about to dash off when she turned back for a moment. 'Marco bought you flowers. Doris put them in a pot.'

'How lovely,' said Joanna, sneezing. 'Oh, drat this cold. Off you go, darling, well away from me and my sneezes.'

'OK.' Polly eyed her anxiously. 'Get better soon, Jo.'

'I will!' Joanna mopped herself up vigorously. 'I'll be fighting fit in a day or two, I promise.'

Marc rang later that night, long after Polly was in bed. 'I wasn't allowed to visit you on your bed of pain,' he said drily. 'Doris appeared to think that one look at you with your red nose and swollen eyes would send me raving mad with lust.'

Joanna giggled. 'I'm sure the thought of lust never crossed Doris's mind——'

'Lucky old Doris.'

There was an awkward pause. 'Thank you for the flowers, by the way,' Joanna said hastily, coughing a little.

'I had hoped to present them in person.'

'Just as well you didn't. I look revolting—and you'd probably have caught my cold.'

'I swore I wouldn't say this, after the way you sent me packing last week, but I missed you today,' he said gruffly. 'Polly did too. She said so in no uncertain terms.'

Joanna gave a shaky sigh. 'It's better this way, Marc.'

'Better for whom, Joanna? It certainly wasn't better for Polly. Nor for me. We were like lost souls without you. So it must have been yourself you were thinking of when you decided to back out of future outings. Own up, Joanna. You're a coward—in a cold funk at the thought of getting involved.'

'I'm not,' she denied, so fiercely it brought on an attack of coughing which rendered her speechless for a while. 'It was Polly I was thinking of,' she went on hoarsely at last.

He laughed scornfully. 'What a load of rubbish, Joanna Swan. You backed out of the arrangement because you're afraid of committing yourself to a normal, healthy relationship where a man's concerned. Polly's just your excuse for running away from me. You're worried I might crack that shell you've been living in, make you feel like a flesh and blood woman in a way Paul Clifford never did.'

'How dare you?' she croaked, incensed.

'I dare because——' He stopped dead. 'Oh, what's the use?' he said fiercely. 'Forget it. I've no right to interfere in your life. Have it your way. Polly's adaptable. She'll just have to accept the failure of her plan.'

'What plan?'

'She thinks it would be nice if the three of us lived together, just like the Lavenhams.' He laughed shortly. 'Don't worry. I explained, in as simple terms as possible, that this wasn't remotely possible. One way and another.'

CHAPTER SEVEN

To HER intense irritation, Joanna, who normally shook off minor complaints with ease, found it hard to get rid of her cold. One of the contributing factors to her slow convalescence, she knew perfectly well, was Marc Anstey's apparent lack of concern. He rang, it was true, but beyond a perfunctory enquiry about her health said nothing personal other than his regret at not being able to take Polly out the following weekend. He was bidden to lunch by the owner of the *Citadel*, an offer he couldn't refuse.

'If I could talk to Polly for a moment I'd like to explain to her personally,' he said with chill courtesy.

Rebuffed, as he very plainly intended, Joanna took the phone along to Polly's bedroom and left the child alone to talk to her uncle.

When Polly came back with the phone Joanna eyed her closely.

'Are you disappointed, darling? Because you won't see your uncle this weekend?'

Polly nodded, mouth drooping. She heaved a big sigh. 'But Marco said I must be a big girl and understand. He'll come next week. Without *fail*,' she added, in touching reproduction of Marc's forceful manner.

That night Joanna woke with a start. She turned on her bedside lamp to find a tearful little figure standing beside the bed.

'Can I come in your bed?' sobbed Polly.

'Oh, darling, of course you can.' Joanna turned back the covers in welcome, scooping the child into the warm bed. Joanna held Polly tightly, rubbing her cheek over the damp, tangled curls.

'What is it?' she asked gently. 'Are you missing your Mamma?'

Polly nodded, sniffing hard. 'But Marco said she's happy in heaven 'cos I'm safe with you.'

Joanna's throat tightened. 'Did he, darling?'

Polly gave a huge, shaky sigh. 'I just wish Marco could live here too with you 'n' me 'n' Sunny.'

'He can't do that, Polly, because he works in London. You know he's got an important new job?'

Polly smiled proudly. 'Yes. Marco's clever.' She eyed Joanna sternly. 'Why don't you like him, Jo?'

Joanna tried to smile. 'But I do.'

Polly frowned. 'Then why——?' She bit her lip, suddenly the picture of guilt.

Joanna eyed her narrowly. 'Why what, Paola Anstey?'

'Marco said not to.'

'Out with it!'

Polly buried her head against Joanna's shoulder. 'Why won't you let Marco live here? Then we'd be like the twins and their mummy and daddy.'

Joanna lay very still, staring at the ceiling, sending up a silent prayer for guidance before doing her best to explain to Polly that the way things were would just have to do. That not everyone had a family like the Lavenhams.

'Just remember, Polly,' she added, 'that your Marco loves you very much and so do I. But your uncle and I hardly know each other. Grown-ups don't live together until they know each other very well.'

'I live with you, and you haven't known me long,' said Polly unanswerably.

'That's different,' said Joanna firmly, and put the light out. 'Now go to sleep, my cherub, or you won't keep awake in school tomorrow.'

The locations for Snowbird's adventures varied with the seasons. In summer his escapades took place at the beach, but now Joanna painted him against a background of autumn leaves and bonfires, Hallowe'en and Guy Fawkes night. Ignoring her cold, she worked hard while Polly was in school, and at the weekend let the child set up her new easel and drawing-board in the study so they could work together. And as the time went by Joanna convinced herself that her life was full. That it lacked nothing that Marc Anstey could provide.

Marc rang fairly regularly, it was true, but these days it was all too obvious that he'd taken the hint, that he now considered Joanna's role in his life minimal. As far as he was concerned, he made it clear, her sole function was a means of communication with Polly. To Joanna's shame she had to curb a strong urge to eavesdrop on their talks, even to question the child about them afterwards. Then one night, before asking to speak to Polly, he made a suggestion which filled Joanna with sharp dismay.

'As you know,' he said impersonally, 'I start at the *Citadel* soon. Since I'm likely to be tied up rather a lot from then on, while I get to grips with the new job, I thought that instead of just lunching with Polly next Sunday as originally planned I'd take her away for a holiday next week.'

'Away?' said Joanna, dismayed. 'Where?'

'To a Greek island called Chyros. A friend of mine owns a house there. I thought a few days in the sun would do Polly good. And you could have a good rest while she's off your hands,' he added. 'You still sound a bit hoarse. Cold still hanging on?'

'No,' snapped Joanna. 'I'm fine.'

'Good. Would you pack a few things for Polly, then, please? I'll come for her on Friday night.'

'Certainly. Would you like to speak to Polly now—describe the delights in store?'

'Do I detect a hint of sarcasm?'

'I'll just take the phone in to her,' said Joanna distantly. 'She's reading in bed. Goodbye.'

Polly was so excited at the prospect of the holiday that she was hard to handle for the next few days. Joanna would have been hard put to cope with the child if Jack and Charlie Lavenham hadn't come round after school to play with her most days. The twins were deeply envious of Polly's forthcoming trip to the sun.

'As well they might be,' said Mary cheerfully. 'My darling husband's stipend doesn't run to exotic holidays, I'm afraid. And George's principles won't allow him to use any of my money for things like that.'

Mary, the cherished only daughter of comfortably off parents, had been left a considerable private income, which was, in her words, as much use as a sick headache due to her husband's scruples.

'George refuses to use it for anything other than eventual school fees.' Mary sighed. 'He even vetoes raids on my piggy-bank for fripperies like a reliable car, or a few miles of new curtain for the Rectory windows.'

Joanna chuckled. 'He let you buy a new cooker.'

'Ah, yes, but George, saint though he be, loves his food. I said, "No cooker, George, no meals." End of problem.'

Joanna got to her feet as the noise volume increased upstairs, but Mary waved her back. 'Relax. You only charge off when there's a deadly hush, love.' She eyed Joanna searchingly. 'I say, Jo. You look a bit washed out. Cold still bothering you?'

'No.' Joanna topped up their coffee-cups. 'I suppose if I'm honest I hate the thought of Polly going off to Greece next week. I'll miss her.'

Mary, who with her George was the only one in Joanna's confidence regarding Polly, eyed her friend thoughtfully. 'You really adore that child, don't you? I don't know that I could have been so noble under the circumstances.'

'Of course you could,' scoffed Joanna. 'Besides, I don't have much else to fill my life, other than Snowbird, do I? Polly's a handful sometimes, but she's a loving little soul. The house will seem empty while she's away. Thank heavens for the dog.'

'The twins tell me Polly would like her uncle to move into Swan House with you—provide her with a ready-made family,' announced Mary, then stared as Joanna flushed to the roots of her hair. 'Oh, dear. I've struck a nerve.'

Joanna pulled a face. 'Actually it's all your fault. Polly yearns for a family just like yours. She had to be enlightened, as gently as possible, that it just isn't on.'

'How did Marc Anstey feel about it?'

'I'm afraid I'm more concerned with my own feelings—and Polly's of course—than his.' Joanna sighed gloomily. 'We can't play happy families just because she wants us to. Besides,' she added bitterly. 'My experience of happy families isn't exactly extensive, is it, what with my defecting mother—and Paul.'

'Paul's dead now,' said Mary sharply. 'And you're much too young, Joanna, to turn your back on all possibility of a family of your own.' She leaned forward to pat Joanna's hand. 'I know your accident put paid to any more babies, but surely if you marry again you could adopt a child? Polly's a darling, but you can't devote your entire life to her. To be blunt, you could do with a man in your life. Some women function perfectly happily without the blighters, I know, but don't kid me you're one of them.'

Joanna smiled, filled with a sudden urge to confide. 'I'm not. I fancy Polly's arrangement like mad, if you must know, Mary.' She smiled wryly as Mary's brown eyes rounded in astonishment. 'If I followed my baser instincts I'd let Marc Anstey into my life, my bed, anywhere he cares to be. But with Polly to consider it's out of the question. Love affairs end. And if I had an affair with Marc who would be the one to suffer most when it was over? Polly! So I'm not going to let it start.'

When Marc arrived to collect Polly late on Friday afternoon Joanna was so determined to conceal her pleasure at seeing him that her greeting was glacial.

'Everything's packed and ready,' she said, while Polly hugged her tall uncle. 'Not having much idea of the climate on this island of yours, I've put in a selection of clothes. Plus a first-aid kit with various medications Polly might need.'

'It's a Greek island, Joanna, not the wilds of Borneo!'

'It's best to make sure. Can I give you tea, or coffee?'

'Thank you. Tea sounds good.' Marc, looking drawn and sombre as he sat down at the kitchen table, watched Polly playing with the dog while Joanna filled a kettle and clattered teacups on a tray. He looked up. 'You're very pale,' he commented.

'I've been burning the midnight oil to meet a deadline.'

Polly chimed in eagerly to tell Marc about the Snowbird stories. 'Jo tells them to me first,' she added importantly.

'I'd like to see one of them,' said Marc.

'Can I get some from the study, Jo?' demanded Polly, jumping to her feet in excitement.

'Of course.' Joanna poured tea with a steady hand then passed a dish of home-made strawberry jam for Marc to spread on scones still warm from the oven.

He ate and drank in silence for a moment, watching her abstractedly. 'You know, Joanna, the life I lead tends to make me forget that there are places like this, with people like you, who cook proper food and stop for tea, where life is a calm, pleasant affair instead of the rat-race I lead.'

'Before Polly came to live with me I never had tea,' she said, smiling a little. 'But now it's a ritual when we get back from school in the afternoon. Children get used to rituals *very* quickly,' she added with emphasis.

Marc stared at her moodily. 'Possibly. But I still don't see why the three of us couldn't go out together occasionally. Dammit, Joanna, Polly's old enough to understand that it doesn't have to mean a permanent arrangement——' He stopped dead. 'Sorry. Didn't mean to bore you with all that again. And don't worry. I'll take very good care of her. I can't promise afternoon tea on a Greek island, but I'll do my best otherwise—— ' He broke off as Polly returned, staggering under a pile of large, hardback picture books containing as many of the adventures of Snowbird as she could carry. 'Careful, *cara*, you'll do yourself a mischief—give them to me.'

With Polly hovering at his elbow Marc went through the pile of books, Joanna watching on tenterhooks as he skimmed through one after another without comment.

'I've seen these displayed in bookshops,' he said at last, looking up. 'I didn't know then, of course, that you were Joanna Swan. They're magical. I congratulate you. It's not often that something as artistic as these is so commercially viable.'

Joanna relaxed, concealing her intense pleasure at his praise.

'They're great fun to do, but after this batch Snowbird's going out to grass, I'm afraid. He's had quite a run, but it's over now.'

'Have you anything in mind to take his place?'

She nodded. 'I quite fancy trying my hand at an adult novel. I created Snowbird to get Saladin out of my system. As a kind of catharsis, I suppose. Now I feel ready to tackle something different.'

Marc glanced at Polly, who was gazing at Joanna, drinking in every word. 'Are you ready, *tesoro*? Nearly time to go.'

When Polly had skipped upstairs Marc turned back to Joanna. 'If your Snowbird books were a way of getting your horse out of your system, what's the motivation for your novel? Will that be based on experience, or complete fiction?'

'A combination of both, I imagine. Isn't that how most writers function? You're the journalist. You must know how it works.'

'I'm mainly a hard news man. I don't go much for fiction.' Marc got up, holding out his hand. 'Goodbye, then, Joanna.'

She looked at the outstretched hand, afraid to touch it in case the contact breached the wall of reserve she'd constructed so carefully against him.

Marc eyed her derisively as his hand fell to his side. 'I forgot. Touching's against the rules, of course.'

'Marc——' she began impulsively, moving towards him, then stopped as Polly came running into the kitchen.

'Ready!' she cried happily. She dropped on her knees to cuddle Sunny, planting kisses on his smooth gold head. 'Be a good boy for Jo, Sunny.' She jumped up and threw herself in Joanna's arms, hugging her tightly. 'I wish you were coming too.'

So did Joanna, the urge so sudden and overwhelming that she buried her face in Polly's curls, afraid Marc might tune in to it. 'I'll be here when you come back. Have fun, darling.' She smiled brightly at Marc. 'Enjoy your holiday.'

'I'll try.' He picked up Polly's luggage, his black eyes narrowed as they met Joanna's. 'Take it easy while we're away. You look very pale.'

She shrugged, smiling brightly. 'I'm fine, honestly.'

There were more hugs and kisses from Polly before Marc could get her in his car. Joanna waved them off, her face lint-white under the porch light as the car moved off down the drive, then went back into a house which suddenly felt very empty and still.

Joanna was grateful for Sunny's company when Polly had gone. The Lavenhams had taken advantage of half-term to spend most of the week with George's parents, leaving Joanna with Doris as her only contact with the outside world.

Joanna missed Polly more than she would have believed possible. In a few short weeks the child had invaded Swan House and Joanna's heart to such an extent that she felt like a lost soul with only herself for company. After two days of solitude Joanna was utterly delighted to receive a phone call from Chyros, but Marc managed only a word or two before Polly's excited voice was chattering in Joanna's ear about the flight and the boat to the island and the little white house right by the sea.

When Joanna put the phone down the house seemed lonelier than ever, deciding her to take Sunny for a walk into Swancote to buy stamps. In the post office stores Mrs Birkin the post-mistress introduced Joanna to the doctor who'd recently gone into partnership with Dr Penfold, the man who'd brought Joanna into the world. Roger Morley was very pleasant, large and fair with a re-assuring air about him which appealed to Joanna very much.

'I hope you enjoy living in Swancote,' she said as he opened the door for her.

'I'm sure I shall,' he said, bending to pat Sunny's head as Joanna unfastened the leash from the railing outside. 'I'm glad of the chance to meet you, Mrs Clifford. I've just moved in to old Mr Reynolds' house just down the road from you. I'm your new neighbour.'

Joanna smiled warmly. 'So you're the mystery purchaser! The village jungle drums must be on the blink. I didn't know who bought it. Let me know if there's anything your wife needs. I'll call round when you're settled and introduce myself.'

Roger Morley looked a trifle embarrassed. 'Afraid I'm divorced. I live alone these days.' He smiled ruefully. 'Nevertheless I hope you and your husband will drop in for a drink one evening.'

'Actually, Dr Morley, I'm a widow. A fairly recent one,' Joanna added, to offset any hint of invitation he might have read into her statement. 'There's just me and my little ward, Polly, at Swan House. And Sunny, of course.' With a friendly smile she said goodbye and walked home briskly, pleased that her new neighbour was so pleasant.

Joanna renewed her onslaught on her work with determination, set on despatching the final Snowbird adventures to her editor as soon as possible. When Marc brought Polly back she intended to concentrate on the child. The new project could wait for a while. There was no financial problem now to provide a spur. She could afford to take it easy for a while, get herself thoroughly fit.

Joanna worked like a maniac for three days, breaking off only to let Sunny out into the garden now and then, and to take him for a longish walk each afternoon. She met Roger Morley more than once during these excursions, and stopped to chat for a minute or two, aware that he'd have lingered longer each time if given the least encouragement. He was lonely, Joanna knew. Moving into a new house alone had to be a rather depressing experience, with no one to see if he was hanging the pictures straight or how the furniture should be arranged. He was a very attractive man, she thought ruefully, wondering why her reaction to him was so negative compared with her response to Marc, who had only to come through the door for her hormones to start dancing a highland fling.

Two days before the holidaymakers were due to return Joanna packed up the finished manuscripts in triumph, walked with Sunny to the village to post them off, then did nothing much at all for the rest of the day. And that night she slept more soundly than she had for months, secure in the knowledge that her deadline had been met with time to spare, and that now all her attention could be focused on getting herself and the house in welcoming mood, ready for Marc's and Polly's return.

Joanna was ready hours before Marc was due to arrive with Polly. She'd baked Polly's favourite cake, helped Doris with the house, taken Sunny for a walk, until at last there was nothing left to do but wait. She knew she looked better than she had done in a long time. Deadline or not, the break on her own had done her good as Marc had forecast it would. Now her cold was finally a thing of the past her hair shone with a healthy gloss, and her skin glowed very satisfactorily against the apricot wool of her sweater. Joanna found it hard to fill the time until the appointed hour arrived. When the hour passed with no sign of Marc and Polly she switched on the television to check the teletext section which listed flight arrivals, horrified to find that their plane, far from crashing, had landed on time. Marc should have arrived with Polly long since. Joanna began pacing up and down like a caged tigress, frantic with worry, almost jumping out of her skin when the long-awaited ring of the telephone finally interrupted her.

She leapt across the room to seize the receiver. 'Marc?'

'Is this Mrs Joanna Clifford?' asked a crisp female voice.

Joanna sagged with disappointment. 'Yes.'

'Swanford General here, Casualty Department.'

Joanna went cold. 'Yes?' she said hoarsely.

'We have a Mr Marcantonio Anstey here.'

Marcantonio? thought Joanna, dazed.

'There was an accident on the bypass. Mr Anstey is only slightly hurt, but——'

'Polly?' said Joanna urgently. 'He had a little girl with him, Paola, his niece.'

'Don't worry, she's fine. Shaken, and very bewildered, of course, and crying for you, Mrs Clifford, but she was in the back of the car, asleep.

Mr Anstey suffered slight cuts and bruises, and possibly a mild concussion. He's not fit to drive. Can you come to fetch them? I gather they were due to arrive at your house some time ago.'

'I'll come at once,' said Joanna tersely. 'Thank you.'

Joanna shut Sunny in the kitchen, pulled on a jacket and ran outside to the garage. Blessing the fact that Swanford General was only ten miles away, she drove as fast as she dared, thankful the bypass was relatively quiet by this time. At the hospital she parked the car as near the Casualty entrance as possible, and raced inside, blind to the curious glances of people waiting for treatment. The woman at the reception desk looked up with a reassuring smile as Joanna gave her name.

'Ah, yes, Mrs Clifford. Mr Anstey's just having his wound stitched. Staff Nurse is with Polly in one of the offices.'

Joanna hurried after the receptionist to a small room where a pretty nurse was cuddling Polly on her lap. The child turned as the door opened, her tearful face lighting up like a lamp as she leapt from the nurse's knee into Joanna's outstretched arms, clinging to her like a limpet, burrowing her face into Joanna's neck. 'Marco's hurt,' she sobbed brokenly. 'Will he die, Jo?'

'Goodness me, no,' said the staff nurse calmly. 'Why would he do that? You're uncle's got a wee cut on his forehead and the doctor's making it better right this minute. He can go home with you soon.'

Joanna gave warm thanks to the nurse, who excused herself to go back to work. Joanna sat down with Polly on her lap, smiling down into the woebegone little face. 'Goodness, you're brown. Did you have a good time?'

Polly nodded, sniffing. 'But I wish you'd been there, Jo.'

Joanna hugged her, then put Polly away a little to cough suddenly. 'Sorry, poppet,' she gasped, surprised. 'I haven't coughed in ages.'

The staff nurse popped her head back round the door. 'Mr Anstey's ready, Mrs Clifford. One of the porters will come with you to the car.'

Joanna took Polly by the hand to follow the staff nurse along to one of the curtained cubicles where Marc sat waiting, the dressing on his forehead standing out starkly against a tanned face embellished with several minor cuts and a shiner of a black eye.

'Hello, Marc,' said Joanna, restraining Polly's desire to hurl herself at her uncle. 'Ready to go home?'

'Sorry about this, Joanna.' He smiled ruefully as he took Polly's hand. 'We were unlucky. Some maniac ran into the back of us while we were waiting to get off the bypass on to the Swanford roundabout. Polly woke up with a fright, and I shot against the windscreen. The belt prevented any serious damage, but my car's in a mess.'

'Never mind the car. You're both safe, which is all that matters.' She smiled at him. 'Let's go home.'

Joanna drove very slowly on the way back to Swancote, afraid Polly might be nervous after the recent trauma, but to her surprise Polly chattered like a magpie all the way, recounting the glories of the Greek holiday, and bewailing, several times, the fact that Jo hadn't been there. Marc made no effort to join in the conversation. His explanation at the hospital appeared to have exhausted his powers of speech.

'The nurse said you might feel drowsy,' warned Joanna when they arrived at Swan House. She steadied Marc as he got out of the car, unable to stifle a cough as the cold night air hit her chest.

Marc stood straight with an effort. 'Still coughing, I see.'

'I haven't been lately,' she said briskly. 'Probably a combination of this cold wind and the nasty shock you two gave me.' She grabbed at him. 'Steady! You're wavering all over the place. For heaven's sake forget your manly pride and lean on me, Marc. We'll go the back way, it's nearer. Here's the key, Polly. Can you unlock the door?'

Polly nodded eagerly, eventually managing to open the door at the third attempt. She gave a cry of joy as Sunny hurled himself towards her in tumultuous welcome, and Joanna left them to their ecstatic reunion to support Marc though the hall and into the drawing-room, where he collapsed in relief on the sofa, breathing hard.

'Hell, I'm sorry about this Joanna,' he panted. 'I knew you'd be off your head with worry, but there was no way I could get a message to you sooner.'

'Never mind. You're here now, not exactly in one piece, but it could have been a lot worse.' Joanna piled cushions behind him, then swung his feet up so that he was lying more comfortably. 'You stay quiet for a bit while I give Polly some supper.'

'She had a few bits and pieces on the plane.' He managed a smile. 'She's been so good, Joanna.'

'I'm sure she has. Have a nap. I'll feed Polly in the kitchen.'

Now Polly knew her beloved Marco wasn't about to join Mamma in heaven she ate quite a hearty supper. Grateful for the amazing resilience of the young, Joanna gave Polly a glass of milk, told her to say goodnight to Sunny, then took her to see Marc before going to bed.

His eyes opened as Polly approached on tiptoe, his smile tender as he held out his arms. Polly embraced him with exquisite care, asking anxiously if he was hurting.

'Only a little bit, *tesoro*. Off you go to bed. It's late. I'll see you in the morning.' Marc kissed her on both cheeks then patted her bottom. 'Be a good girl for Joanna.'

Polly looked indignant as she took Joanna's hand. 'O'course I will. 'Night, Marco.'

Joanna let Polly get away without a bath for once. Tonight it seemed more important to get the child tucked up in her bed and asleep than to fuss over whether she was clean or not. Afterwards, in her bedroom for some necessary repairs to her face, Joanna began coughing again. Crossly she decided it must be psychosomatic, and drank some water, then a spoonful of the linctus Doris had brought while the cold was in full force. But cough or not, a look in the mirror confirmed that her earlier glow was surprisingly undimmed by the trauma of the evening. Just to have Marc here in the house with her again seemed to have ignited a visible light inside her.

Joanna returned quietly to the drawing-room to find Marc deeply asleep, his face exhausted above the blood-stained white sweater. The dressing stood out, stark against his tan, the bruise around his eye darker already, giving him a raffish look Joanna found dangerously irresistible. Snatching back the hand which yearned to stroke his cheek, she tiptoed from the room to join Sunny in the kitchen. Not sure what sort of eating mood Marc would be in when he woke up, Joanna cut slices of ham, laid a tray, then collected the book she was reading and went back to the drawing-room to curl up in a chair until Marc woke.

In the warmth and peace of the familiar room reaction suddenly hit Joanna like a body blow. Limp as a rag doll, she leaned her head against the cushion, gazing at Marc's sleeping face as it dawned on her that he'd have to stay the night. Whatever his original intention had been, to drive back to London, or even spend the night at the Lamb and Flag, there was no question of his doing either now. Joanna closed her eyes, a shiver running through her as she thought of how much worse it could all have been. She sat erect, limp no longer, as it struck her that if Marc had been killed she would probably have spent the rest of her life regretting the way she'd kept him at arm's length. She closed her eyes and wriggled back down in the chair, giving way to fatigue which engulfed her so completely that she was soon as deeply asleep as her companion.

Joanna woke to a rough tongue licking her cheek, and shot upright in the chair, blinking up at Marc owlishly as she pushed Sunny away. She jumped to her feet guiltily.

'I must have dropped off. Is it late? I'm sorry——'

'Relax.' Marc grinned, looking a different man after his rest. 'I'd have let you sleep, but this chap was making a fuss in the kitchen, so I took him for a stroll outside. He got back in here to you before I could stop him.'

'A good thing he did!' Joanna pushed at her hair, self-conscious under his amused gaze. 'I'll get you something to eat.'

'Good,' he said cheerfully. 'I could eat a horse.'

Joanna eyed the clock in consternation. 'Heavens, it's past eleven! You must be starving. How do you feel?'

'My head's a bit sore, but I don't feel sick any more.' He smiled as he strolled after her to the kitchen. 'My skull's too thick to succumb to a little bump like that.'

Joanna grinned as she made sandwiches. 'You said that, not me! Sorry, by the way. These are ham, not horse.'

They sat together at the kitchen table, Marc making short work of the food as he gave Joanna a graphic account of the holiday, and how Polly had loved the little sugar-cube house on Chyros. But once Sunny was settled down for the night, and they were back in the drawing-room, the atmosphere altered abruptly.

Marc shot a sombre glance at Joanna as she handed him a cup of coffee. 'I'm sorry about to-night—giving you a shock like that. You took it very well, and I'm grateful.'

'The accident wasn't your fault. Thank heaven it was no worse.' She looked worried. 'But I hope it won't have a delayed-action effect on Polly. It's a wonder she set foot in the car again tonight, on top of what happened to Rosa.'

'Polly doesn't know about the car crash. Rosa died in hospital, so Polly believes her mother was just taken ill, and went to heaven. That's why she gets so uptight about illness in any form.' He shrugged wearily. 'Maybe I was wrong, but at the time it seemed best to keep the truth from her.'

'You were very definitely right,' said Joanna emphatically. 'Otherwise she wouldn't have been so good about coming home in the car tonight straight after the bump.'

'That's because you were driving. She doesn't associate danger or harm with you, Joanna.' His eyes moved over her face broodingly. 'I can't say I feel the same way.'

There was a sudden, fraught silence.

'What do you mean?' asked Joanna at last.

'Don't pretend, Joanna. You know you've been a danger to my peace of mind from the moment I first set eyes on you.' He went on looking at her, until Joanna kept from fidgeting only by sheer strength of will.

'The spare bed is made up,' she said in a strained voice.

One of Marc's slim black eyebrows rose mockingly. 'You mean you're actually allowing me to sleep beneath your roof?'

'What do you expect me to do?' she demanded angrily. 'Turn you out in the snow?'

Marc smiled sardonically. 'You'd probably like to.'

'I wouldn't turn anyone out in your particular state of health,' she said sharply, and got to her feet. 'I'm sure you're tired. If you can manage to carry your bag up I'll show you where you're to sleep.'

'If necessary,' said Marc silkily as he hefted his hold-all, 'I could carry you upstairs as well as the bag, concussion or no concussion, but don't be nervous. I shan't make the attempt.'

Joanna gave him a kindling look, then stalked out of the room ahead of him, slowing down as she mounted the stairs for fear of waking Polly. Marc followed close behind, pausing beside her as they looked in on Polly who lay, arms outflung in total abandon, so deeply asleep that a regiment of soldiers could have marched along the landing without waking her.

'She's worn out,' Joanna whispered as she showed Marc to the spare room.

Marc put down his bag at the end of the bed, then turned to face her. 'Thank you, Joanna, for everything. I truly appreciate your coming to rescue us tonight. I'm sorry I needled you just now. Lord knows you've had a lot to contend with from me and mine lately. You were a wonder tonight.'

Joanna shrugged as she went to the door. 'I just did what anyone else would have done. I hope you sleep well. Goodnight.'

'Goodnight.' He smiled, looking dark and alien, his villainous black eye incongruous against the faded chintz of the Swan House guest-room.

Sure she'd lie awake all night, Joanna fell asleep almost at once, even though Marc lay only a few feet away on the other side of her bedroom wall. But as the temperature dropped in the night her room grew cold and her cough returned to plague her. She woke herself violently at last and shot up in bed, gasping for breath. She switched on her lamp, then stared, her eyes dilating, as Marc slid silently into the room and closed the door behind him.

'Medicine?' he whispered.

Joanna, hand clapped to her mouth, pointed speechlessly to the bottle on the bedside table. Marc measured a dose into the plastic cup beside it then stood over her while she swallowed the linctus down. She tried to smile her thanks, flustered suddenly because his short robe revealed so much long brown leg.

He looked at her questioningly. 'All right, Joanna?'

She nodded wordlessly.

'I've looked in on Polly. She's still out for the count.'

'Thank you.' Joanna swallowed, her eyes on a level with Marc's bronzed chest, her pulse racing as she saw he was breathing unevenly. Slowly, like someone hypnotised, she raised her blank blue eyes to his, and they stared at each other, spellbound, Joanna motionless against the pillows, Marc rooted to the spot. Then Marc let out a great unsteady sigh. As though some giant fist had pushed him from behind he dropped on his knees beside the bed and pulled her into his arms, kissing her like a man at the end of his tether.

Joanna yielded to him without reservation, rejoicing. To feel Marc's lips against hers, the warmth of his lean body, was sheer heaven after the agony, however brief, of believing he'd been killed. She would have told him so if her mouth hadn't been so ravishingly otherwise employed. It seemed so much more important to pull him closer, to welcome him into her bed, than talk. Then Joanna forgot Polly, forgot everything, as a tidal wave of sheer need submerged them both the instant their bodies came into contact. Every nerve in her system leapt in response to Marc's urgency, gloriously in tune with his consuming urge to celebrate life after his brush with danger. He raised his head, his eyes glittering with a question Joanna answered without words, her smile radiant with shared delight.

'I always knew,' he whispered victoriously, as his hands slid in a lazy, lingering caress down her hips. 'Right from the first, I *knew*.'

'Knew what?' She shivered, her eyelids suddenly heavy.

'How it would be for us.' His kisses grew ravenous, his hands moving over her in triumphant possession as his fingertips blazed a trail of fire over her breasts and hips and thighs. But even as his caresses grew wilder Joanna knew, beyond all doubt, that he was deliberately withholding the moment of union until her desire was as great as his.

Nothing in Joanna's experience had prepared her for such bliss. Having been married to a man too concerned with his own pleasure to care much about hers, she now responded in astonished delight to Marc's slightest touch, returning his kisses with an ardour which tested his control to the limit. Her body moved restlessly beneath his, her fingers knotting in the damp curls on his chest, digging into the skin sheathing his shoulder muscles until at last, tantalised beyond bearing, she resorted to a caress so intimate that he was vanquished.

'*Diletta mia,*' he groaned. The breath left Joanna's body as they came together in a long, sustained assault on the senses, and Marc let out a great, shuddering sigh, burying his face against her throat as their bodies united in a fierce, rhythmic quest for fulfilment.

Joanna came back to earth to the touch of Marc's mouth on her damp eyelids, of his hands stroking her back as he held her against him, whispering gratifying things in her ear instead of flopping over on his back and falling asleep, as Paul had always done.

'How do you feel?' she murmured drowsily.

He laughed, rippling a fingertip down her spine. 'How do you think I feel, woman? Amazed, ecstatic——'

'I *meant*,' said Joanna, pulling away slightly, 'how's your head?'

Marc put up a hand to his forehead in surprise. 'Now you come to mention it, it's throbbing a bit. One way and another I forgot about it before.' He grinned. 'How's your cough?'

She buried her face against his shoulder to stifle her laughter. 'Conspicuous by its absence.'

Marc stuck an ungentle finger under her chin. 'Have you missed me?' he demanded.

'Not in the least,' she lied, giving him a feline little smile. 'In fact I've been seeing quite a lot of Roger.'

His eyes narrowed. 'Who the hell's Roger?'

'The new doctor here, Roger Morley. He's charming.'

'Has he taken you out?'

'No,' she admitted. 'I just meet him now and then when I'm walking Sunny.'

Marc shook her slightly. 'Enjoy making me fry, don't you?'

'Were you frying?'

'You know I was.' He kissed her savagely, his hands sliding round to cup her breasts, 'I'm jealous of any man allowed in your vicinity, if you want the naked truth, Joanna Swan. I may be a civilised Brit on the surface, but scratch it and you soon get down to my Sicilian ancestry.' He bent his head to take a sharply pointing nipple between his lips, the ensuing sensation so exquisite that Joanna forgot her tart rejoinder, bowled over by the astonishing discovery that, far from being a one-off, her experience of love at Marc Anstey's clever hands was not only about to be repeated, but surpassed.

'Well, that's that, I suppose,' she sighed eventually, when they lay at rest at last in each other's arms.

'That's what?'

'Well, if you'd made love to me once I could have passed it off to myself as an accident. Circumstances beyond my control and all that. But twice in a row . . .' She shook her head, smiling at him.

He propped himself up on an elbow to look down at her. 'Will you believe that much as I wanted you I'd have stopped if you'd called a halt at any stage?'

'Oh, I know that. I suppose, in a way, that's why it happened. I never felt threatened.' She smiled demurely. 'I could tell you wanted me, of course——'

'Full marks for observation!'

Joanna grinned. 'But at the same time I knew you'd never use force to get your wicked way.'

Marc smoothed her hair back from her flushed face. 'Forcing a woman is not my style, *carissima*.' He smiled crookedly. 'Not, I feel obliged to point out, that it's ever been necessary.'

She gave him a dig in the ribs. 'Bighead!'

'Why *did* you let me make love to you, Joanna?' he asked, suddenly very serious. 'What changed your mind?'

Joanna's eyes burned darkly blue with candour. 'When the hospital phoned I thought you'd been killed.'

'The police would have come to tell you that.'

'I know that—who better? But don't forget I'd been worried sick for ages before I heard from the hospital. In the second before I knew what happened——' She shuddered, and he pulled her close.

'I was a coward before, you see,' she went on huskily after a while. 'That's why I sent you away. I was attracted to you so quickly, so—so violently, that the rapport between us scared me to death. I'd never felt like that in my life. I thought it was too sudden, too soon. If only you and I'd been involved it would have been different, but I was afraid of it, sure that if we became lovers it would burn itself out and then Polly would be hurt. So I pushed you away, and you stayed away and I tried to tell myself it was for the best.'

Marc let out a long, unsteady breath. 'Joanna, I want to know exactly how you felt when you thought I was dead.'

'It was only then,' she began, taking her courage in both hands, 'that I learned how I should have felt when Paul was killed. And didn't.'

His arms tightened convulsively. 'Then why were you so hellish distant tonight? You were fine during supper, but afterwards down came the shutters again, closing me out. Oh, no, you don't,' Marc added, holding her fast when she tried to free herself.

'It suddenly occurred to me that you might not be interested any more,' she murmured awkwardly. 'I got cold feet.'

'Are they cold now?'

'No.'

'I should hope not.' Marc held her face cupped in his hands, forcing her to meet his eyes. 'Listen, Joanna Swan. What happened between us just now was just one part—a very wonderful part—of a great many things I feel for you. Of course I *want* you, but I care for you, too. I want to make you happy, make sure you're never hurt again.' He smiled, the light in his eyes melting her utterly. 'Now tell me how you feel about me.'

'Isn't it obvious?' she said crossly. 'Otherwise, Marc Anstey, I would have sent you packing the minute I'd swallowed my medicine.'

Marc's eyes glittered in triumph. 'Does this mean you've changed your mind? About the three of us living together and making Polly's dream come true?'

'Yes.' She smiled, stretching luxuriously. 'Only it'll have to be a weekend arrangement, as far as you're concerned.'

'I'll settle for that,' he said, smoothing back her hair. 'Most people in my sort of job sweat it out alone in London during the week and go home to the country for weekends with the family.' He grinned. 'You realise your main attraction is this house, of course! Saves me a lot of expense. I'm only sorry I shan't have as much time to spend here as I'd like until I get to grips with the new job.' He kissed her lingeringly, then swung his long legs out of bed and sat up, pulling on his robe. 'Besides, you'd prefer a reasonable time to elapse, I suppose.'

Joanna sat up, pulling the covers up to her chin. 'Reasonable time?' she said blankly.

Marc pushed back his dishevelled hair, wincing as he made contact with his wound. 'You've never pretended to feel like a widow where Paul Clifford's concerned, I know. Nevertheless you can't get away from the fact that he's only been dead for a short time. You're so well known in Swancote that it's only natural you'll want to wait for a while before we actually get married.'

Joanna stared at him in utter dismay. 'Married?'

He frowned at her as he tied the belt around his spare waist. 'Yes. Married.'

'But—but, Marc, we don't have to get *married*!'

His face darkened, one eyebrow lifting ominously. 'Why the hell not?'

'I don't know that I can go through all that a second time. I've done it before, remember, including the "death us do part" bit.' Joanna clasped her hand round her knees above the quilt, gazing at his set face in entreaty. 'Look, Marc, I didn't like being married the first time. Don't let's spoil everything with red tape and legality. Can't we just live together, as Polly wants? No strings, no rules, just being together as much as we can, whenever we can. And because we want to be, not just because a piece of paper entitles us to the privilege!'

Marc's black brows flew together, his eyes cold with disbelief. 'Let me get this straight. Are you telling me you can't face marriage with me?'

Joanna shook her head violently. 'No, of course I'm not. But these days it isn't necessary. In fact,' she pointed out, 'you were the one who referred to it as something to evade!'

'True.' His lips twisted in the parody of a smile. 'Like your late, unlamented husband, I'm a Catholic. For me it must be for life. Until now I'd never found someone I *wanted* for life. I'm paying you the highest compliment a man can give a woman, Joanna.'

Joanna gazed at him beseechingly. 'I know, and I'm deeply honoured, believe me. But I can't, Marc. It wouldn't be fair.'

He sat down on the side of the bed, taking her by the shoulders. 'Fair! What the hell do you mean? I don't think it happens to be *fair* for you to profess some kind of feeling for me one minute, then turn me down the next.' He shook her slightly, his eyes spearing hers. 'Joanna. Are you telling me, in a roundabout way, that you don't want me on a permanent basis?'

She shook her head violently. 'Of course I'm not! When I thought you'd been killed I wanted to die too.'

His eyes glittered in triumph, then dulled. 'If you feel like that, why the hell *won't* you marry me?' he demanded violently.

Joanna gazed at him in entreaty. 'Surely you can see why.'

'No. I can't.' He pulled her into his arms and began to kiss her savagely, but when she forced herself to stay limp in his arms he let them fall and stood up. 'Tell me, then,' he said in a voice so dead Joanna shut her eyes tightly in anguish for a moment.

When she opened them the baffled pain on Marc's face almost tempted her to throw herself into his arms and tell him she'd do anything in the world he wanted, just so they could revert to the happiness they'd shared such a short time before. She resisted the impulse, her eyes bright with unshed tears.

'There's something you've forgotten, Marc. I can't give you children—no, hear me out,' she said firmly as he made a move towards her. 'I know we've got Polly, but you'd never able to have a child of your own.'

Marc hesitated a split second then said roughly, 'That's nonsense. If I can have you—and Polly— that's all I ask.'

Joanna gazed at him in misery. 'You think that now, but one day you could change your mind, find someone able to give you the children I can't, just as Paul did. But he had to remain tied to me—and I to him. I just couldn't bear that a second time.'

Marc seemed to withdraw into himself, turning into a grim, forbidding stranger right before her eyes. 'I suppose there's no point in trying to con-

vince you that it wouldn't happen a second time?'
He gave a short, mirthless laugh. 'Obviously not.
I realise now why I've never proposed to anyone
before. Rejection's bloody hard to take.'

'Oh, Marc, don't! I'm not rejecting *you*. Why
can't we just——?'

'Share bed and board on weekends?' he put in
bitingly. 'No way. I'm not some tame stud, Joanna.
If you don't fancy marriage, fair enough, that's
your choice. But as far as I'm concerned it's the
only thing on offer. My aim was to share the rest
of my life with you, not just a bed now and then.'
Marc glanced at his watch. 'I'd better get back to
your spare room. Under the circumstances it would
never do for Polly to discover me in yours. She'd
assume her plan was in full working order, poor
little scrap. Goodnight, Joanna—or good morning,
I suppose. It's nearly dawn.'

Tears streamed down Joanna's face as he crossed
the room. She saw his slim brown hand clench on
the white porcelain of the doorknob as he waited
to give her time to call him back. When she said
nothing he went from the room as quietly as he'd
arrived, leaving her alone with her tears, but
drearily certain she was right. A man had a right
to a family of his own. She could never give Marc
a child. And she loved him too much to tie him
down to a relationship which might turn into a
prison once the first flush of physical attraction died
away. As inevitably it would. Paul had taught her
that particular lesson all too well.

CHAPTER EIGHT

AFTER A whole week with her beloved Marco in the Greek sunshine Polly was philosophical about his subsequent absence from Swan House. He'd told her, she explained to Joanna, that his new job would keep him very busy for a while. Not even his departure early on the morning after their dramatic return troubled Polly too much. She accepted his explanation at breakfast that he had to return to London by train because his car was being mended, and in her pleasure at playing with Sunny failed to register the constraint between Joanna and Marc over a breakfast neither ate. The arrival of a taxi soon afterwards came as a profound relief Marc only too plainly shared with Joanna. Looking strained, his bruised face colourless beneath its tan, he reiterated formal thanks for her help as he said goodbye.

Joanna forced herself to smile as she repudiated the least need for thanks. 'It was nothing.'

'I'm glad you think so. It was a great deal more than that to me.' He smiled mockingly as colour rose in her face. 'Goodbye, Joanna. Take care of that cough.'

'Goodbye.' Joanna stood at the door, watching as Polly skipped alongside Marc towards the car, held up her arms to be hugged, then blew kisses to her uncle as the taxi bore him away.

* * *

Not for the first time Joanna was obliged to pick up the pieces of a life which had fallen apart. She should, she thought with irony, be expert at it by now.

Years before, when her father was terminally ill, the discovery that very little money went with the legacy of Swan House had been a blow. But Joanna had promised her dying father faithfully that somehow she would find a way to keep the house in the family, and if possible hand it down to her children. She'd been working as a secretary to a merchant banker at the time. After graduating she'd failed to find a post which made use of her art history degree, and in desperation had enrolled on a secretarial course which had landed her a job in the City. The work was never more to her than a means to earn money until she found something more to her taste, but she had enjoyed sharing a flat with two other girls, and had led a fairly hectic social life, met a lot of men, and eventually taken to seeing one of them on a regular basis. When her father had died she'd been shattered, not only by grief, but by the burden of the promise she'd made. Edward, her escort, had defected when Joanna proved poor company in her grief, and in despair at breaking her promise she had been on the point of putting Swan House up for sale when she'd met Paul Clifford.

A self-assured, handsome man in his middle forties, or the prime of life in his own phrase, Paul had taken an immediate fancy to the attractive secretary of the man he'd come to consult. Joanna, smarting from Edward's treatment, had warmed to the mature, self-assured businessman, and ac-

cepted his invitations to dinner, and, as she got to
know him better, confided her problems about
Swan House. Once Paul Clifford learned she was
on the point of selling a country house which had
been in her family for two hundred years he had
acted swiftly, using steamroller tactics to get his own
way. He'd bought Swan House and made it over to
Joanna on condition that she married him, gave up
her job, and set about providing him with a family
in the type of home the ambitious boy from the
East End had wanted all his life.

During the afternoon walk with Polly and the
dog later, Joanna marvelled at the naïveté of the
girl who'd mistaken her gratitude to Paul Clifford
for love. Now she'd met Marc Anstey she knew, at
last, exactly what a lasting adult love should be,
what her life still could be, if she could only bring
Marc round to her point of view.

'Are you sad, Jo?' asked Polly anxiously.

'No, darling, of course not! How could I be sad
when you've come home to me?' Joanna smiled
brightly, blowing her nose. 'This wind is making
my eyes run, that's all.'

'Marco said to look after you,' Polly said importantly. 'Let's go home. Here, Sunny. *Good* boy!'

Mary Lavenham, a lady of discernment where
Joanna was concerned, raised her eyebrows when
she heard Joanna had embarked on a novel. 'I
thought you might have had a rest once you finished off the Snowbird books.'

'I need occupation,' said Joanna firmly.

It was Mary's opinion that Joanna should go out more and meet people. There was Roger Morley for a start, charming, unattached——

'And very, very nice, but that's all, so stop matchmaking,' said Joanna, chuckling.

'That's better. You don't smile much lately.' Mary hesitated. 'This Marc Anstey—has he upset you, love?'

'The boot, dear heart, is on the other foot. I upset him.'

'Irrevocably?'

'Utterly.'

'No resumption of diplomatic relations? Ever, I mean?'

'"Nevermore," quoth the raven."' Joanna accepted another cup of Mary's tea. 'So let's not talk about it.'

Mary dropped the subject obediently, suggesting instead that it would be excellent therapy if Joanna both wrote the script and used her artistic talent to paint the scenery for the school nativity play, ideas which appealed to Joanna very much. When Marc made his weekly telephone call to speak to Polly Joanna requested the formality of his approval regarding his niece's inclusion in the cast as a shepherd.

'Not the starring role? I'm surprised,' said Marc drily, sounding less formal than he normally did of late.

'Ah, but playing a shepherd involves a crook and toy lambs borrowed from the local craft shop!' Joanna informed him. 'It was something of a departure to cast a girl as a shepherd, of course, but because the Lavenham twins form the rest of the trio a point was stretched.'

Marc laughed. 'If Polly's tales about those lads are true I pity the producer of the play.'

'She's a jolly, competent sort of girl. Besides, Mary Lavenham's warned the twins that Father Christmas will cross them off his list if they misbehave.' Joanna hesitated. 'While we're on the subject, Marc,' she said diffidently, 'what shall I tell Polly you're doing at Christmas? You're very welcome to spend it here, of course.' She waited, tense, as Marc took his time to answer.

'That's very good of you,' he said at last. 'But even for Polly I don't think I could endure a jolly family Christmas the way things are. It would only emphasise all too bloody painfully what we're both missing because you refuse to marry me, Joanna.'

'It's not my fault!' she snapped. 'I can't help it if you're bristling with high-flown scruples.'

'Hell and damnation, Joanna——' He stopped, breathing in sharply. 'It was like a kick in the teeth to have you turn me down after—after what happened between us.'

Joanna fought for calm, shattered by his unexpected descent into the personal. 'I'm sorry. But you know exactly why I refused.'

'I take it you haven't changed your mind,' he said grimly.

'Have you?'

'No, I have not.'

'Then it's checkmate.' She sighed. 'Forget it, Marc. What do I tell Polly about Christmas?'

'Nothing. I'll tell her myself next Sunday when I take her out for the day.'

At first Joanna had looked forward to seeing Marc when he collected Polly for the weekly outing, but he very quickly disabused her of any pipe dream about talking him round to her way of thinking. He quite simply gave her no opportunity to talk to him at all. Joanna's sole contact with him was a moment or two when he collected Polly, and another brief encounter when he brought her back.

At first Joanna was devastated. She'd been convinced that meeting Marc face to face would be sure to weaken his resolve. When she found she was very much mistaken she took her cue from Marc and answered his greetings with polite enquiries about his progress in the new job, then retreated into the house with Sunny to avoid looking wistful as the car took her loved ones away.

Once the script was written and the scenery finished for the nativity play, Joanna felt eager to get to grips with the novel she'd had simmering in her brain for months. Polly's arrival in her life had meant consigning the novel to a back burner in her mind for a while, but now Polly was settled Joanna decided nothing was going to stop her getting down to work again. Work which might, if she were lucky, help her to get used to the fact that Marc was never going to change his mind about their relationship.

It was mid-December when Joanna first became aware of a marked lack of enthusiasm for sitting down at her typewriter each day.

'I'm getting lazy, Doris,' she sighed, making a pot of tea instead of starting work as soon as she returned from the morning walk to school with Polly and the dog.

'I wouldn't say that, Mrs Clifford,' said Doris, setting out cups. 'Mrs Lavenham thinks you're working much too hard over your new book.'

'I know!' Joanna shook her head, amused. 'Quite funny coming from a busy clergyman's wife who never has a minute to herself. As we speak she's probably running up the costumes for the play with one hand and making cakes for the Mother's Union tea with the other. I don't know where she gets the energy.'

Joanna's Christmas dilemma had eventually been solved by an invitation from the Lavenhams to join them for the festive meal at the Rectory, along with George's parents and a couple of Mary's elderly relatives.

Marc, when Joanna informed him of the arrangement, asked if he might visit Polly on Christmas Eve to deliver her presents.

'I can hardly absent myself altogether, nor do I want to. On the other hand maybe it's just as well I'm not around for her first Christmas Day without Rosa,' he said sombrely. 'That way she won't have anything to remind her of previous years.'

Joanna's previous years had entailed a skiing trip for the festivities. Surrounded by other people in a smart, impersonal hotel, she and Paul had managed to rub through it without too much friction, while at the same time neatly relieving Paul Clifford of a family Christmas with either wife or mistress.

'Whatever you think best,' she said serenely. 'By all means come down on Christmas Eve.' She hesitated, then before she could think better of it suggested he come to lunch. 'Unless you prefer to take Polly out, of course.'

There was a pause. 'Thank you. I eat so many restaurant meals I'd appreciate some home cooking. But please don't go to any trouble,' he added distantly.

'Oh, I won't,' Joanna assured him. 'Polly and I have to eat lunch, anyway.'

Joanna, obliged to sandwich Christmas shopping in between her writing while Polly was in school, did her best to throw off a growing feeling of malaise, but with no success. She felt irritable with herself. For years she'd suffered nothing worse than an odd cold, yet since Paul's death she'd been nothing like her usual healthy self. Worried she might be sickening for something dangerous to Polly, Joanna was driven at last to seek professional help. After two consecutive visits to Roger Morley, who was taking over more and more of Dr Penfold's patients, she returned home, dazed, feeling worse than ever. She clipped on Sunny's lead and took him for a walk to the Rectory, where Mary took one startled look and led Joanna to a chair at the kitchen table before reaching for the coffee.

'No coffee, thanks,' said Joanna. 'These days I can only manage tea!'

Mary's bright eyes widened as she changed course for the tea caddy. 'Tummy upset?'

Joanna gave a hollow laugh. 'You could say that. I've just been talking to Roger Morley.'

'Good! I told you to encourage him a bit.'

'The visit wasn't social, Mary. I haven't been feeling too good for quite a while. I thought I'd better see about it in case I had something Polly might catch.'

Mary stiffened. She slammed the lid of the teapot and went over to Joanna, putting an arm round her shoulders. 'What's the verdict?'

'If I tell you will you keep it to yourself? Even from George?'

Mary looked terrified. 'Oh, good heavens, love, what's wrong with you?'

'I'm pregnant,' said Joanna, and burst into tears.

'Is that all?' Mary held her close, laughing with relief.

'Aren't you listening?' wailed Joanna. 'I'm going to have a baby.'

'Well, yes, Jo. I know what pregnant means...' Mary's eyes widened suddenly. 'Oh, glory. But I thought you couldn't——'

'So did I,' said Joanna bitterly. 'But it seems I can, after all.'

Mary handed her a sheet of kitchen paper. 'Mop yourself up while I pour. Or shall I raid George's sherry decanter?'

Joanna shuddered. 'No! Tea, please.'

Mary filled two mugs with a brew strong enough to melt the spoon, then looked Joanna over assessingly. 'You don't look very pregnant. Poor Paul. He'd have been so pleased——'

'I doubt it. It doesn't show yet because the baby's not his.'

Mary choked on her tea. 'Oops!' She eyed Joanna warily. 'Who?'

'Marc Anstey.' Joanna beat an impotent fist on the kitchen table, badly startling the dog. 'It was the night of the accident. Neither of us meant it to happen. It—it just did. But even if I'd deliberately set out to seduce him I wouldn't have given a thought to any consequences. Oh, Mary, what on earth am I going to do?'

'I don't see your problem. Just tell the man.'

'If I do he'll insist on marrying me.'

'I should jolly well hope so!'

'It's not as simple as that, Mary. He did ask me, and I turned him down flat because I thought I *couldn't* give him a child.' Joanna heaved a despondent sigh. 'I suggested we just, well, cohabited, but he wouldn't hear of it. Anyway, I can't just do a complete U-turn now and say, "Hi, Marc, guess what? Problem solved. I'm pregnant." He might have changed his mind.'

Joanna went home soon afterwards, turning off to walk in the woods with the dog before returning to Swan House. It was such a silly situation to be in, she thought angrily. She'd sent Marc packing because she couldn't have his child, yet the words would stick in her throat if she tried to tell him that Dr Penfold had been wrong all those years ago. The diagnosis had never been put to the test for the simple reason that once Paul had been told there was no possibility of further children he couldn't bring himself to touch her. Besides, it was more than possible that Marc no longer cared for her in that way any more. Men changed. She knew that better than anyone. On the other hand if she told him she was pregnant Marc's principles might force him to offer marriage whether he still wanted it or not. And that would be worse than anything.

Joanna ground her teeth impotently. If she'd known there was the remotest possibility of getting pregnant she'd never have let Marc near her that night. She whistled to the dog, then smiled bitterly.

Who was she trying to kid? That night she'd given no thought to anything other than the joy of being in Marc's arms.

Joanna strode back to the house in a mood so black that she found it impossible to work on her novel when she got home. The problems of her mythical characters paled into such insignificance beside her own that she flung away from the typewriter in the end and went off to the kitchen to make a cake for Polly's tea. One thing was certain, she thought, as she whipped eggs viciously. Marc would know, sooner or later, whether she told him or not. So would Polly, not to mention the entire population of Swancote. There was no hope of disguising the fact that Joanna Swan's child would appear in the world a sight too long after her husband's death to be his.

That night Joanna lay on a sofa in the drawing-room once Polly was in bed, too listless to do anything other than stare at the television. Very little of the evening's programme registered, and, once she realised the credits were rolling on a play she'd been pretending to watch, Joanna got up to let Sunny out before bedtime. She stopped dead halfway to the door as the announcer on *Newsnight* informed her that later there would be an interview with the new foreign editor of the *Citadel*. Marc Anstey, Washington-based until recently, would give his opinion on the latest governmental crisis brewing in the White House.

Joanna rushed the dog out to the kitchen and let him out in the garden, then switched on the small portable on the kitchen counter, her eyes glued to the screen. When the camera finally focused on

Marc's face she slumped down on a kitchen stool, elbows on the counter, her face propped in her hands as she looked on the face of the man she loved. She listened to the familiar gravelly tones of his voice, deeply impressed by the assurance and quiet authority he brought to the discussion on current US affairs. As time went on Joanna grew more and more depressed. Seeing Marc on screen like this, self-contained and elegant, his views listened to with obvious respect by the presenter, was a bittersweet experience. She was totally unprepared for her reaction to this informed, lucid stranger. Until now Marc Anstey had merely been Polly's uncle, Rosa's brother, even, briefly, her own lover. Now, watching him on the screen, it was impossible to see him as anything other than foreign editor of a national newspaper, a formidable, rather glamorous stranger far remote from Joanna Swan and her embarrassing little problem.

The rest of the time until Christmas flew by at much too swift a rate for Joanna. Polly, excited by school Yuletide preparations, was harder to handle than usual, and loud in her lamentations when she learned her darling Marco was not only unable to witness her performance in the school play, but too busy to see her at all until Christmas Eve.

'Try to make her understand, Joanna,' said Marc, when he made a second phone call later that evening to explain why he'd upset Polly so badly earlier. 'I can't make it again this Sunday because I've finally set up a meeting with a certain foreign diplomat the *Citadel*'s been after for months. The man refuses to talk to anyone but me. I can't pass up the chance of an exclusive for the paper.'

'Of course not,' agreed Joanna. 'When she's calmed down a bit I'll have a chat with her, tell her I'll take photographs at the play so you can see her with her crook.'

'Thank you, Joanna. I'm very grateful.'

'Not at all,' she returned politely. 'Congratulations, by the way. I saw you on *Newsnight*. Very impressive.'

'Thank you. One of the aspects of the job I like least.' He yawned suddenly. 'Sorry. I've only just got home. No working dinner with anyone tonight, praise be. I yearn for an early night.'

Joanna's eyebrows rose. 'It's gone nine. You work a long day.'

'Honesty forces me to admit I don't actually get to my office until mid-morning these days, ready for the morning conference at eleven.'

'Perks of the new job?'

'In a way. But don't get me wrong. I still get up at the crack of dawn to listen to Radio Four, and get through all the morning papers before I drive to work.'

'Sounds gruelling. Are you settling in well in the new flat?'

'It's chaos at the moment; the painters are still in. But I like being nearer to the job.' There was a pause. 'How's your novel coming along, Joanna?'

'Fairly well,' she lied, reluctant to tell him that she was suffering from severe writer's block due to circumstances beyond her control. 'Right. I'll do my best to put Polly in the picture. See you on Christmas Eve, then—unless some story breaks to keep you away, of course,' she added.

'I'll be there,' he said curtly. 'Goodbye, Joanna.'

End of term arrived, and with it the performance of the nativity play, which Joanna watched, smiling widely despite the lump in her throat, as Polly entered stage-left with the twins, beaming. Joanna dodged about, in company with several proud parents, taking photographs during the performance, then presided over a celebration tea-party afterwards at Swan House, with Mary on hand to help with the tearing spirits of the three shepherds.

Once school term was over Joanna occupied Polly with preparations for Christmas, taking her to the local forestry commission centre to buy a newly felled tree, and letting her help with the decorations when the tall tree was installed in a corner of the drawing-room. Joanna kept Polly busy by enlisting her help with every Christmas task possible for the child, who was in a high state of excitement as she wrapped presents for the Lavenhams and Doris and her beloved uncle.

Joanna had taken her to Oxford to shop the previous Saturday, and the result, a dark red cashmere scarf with a famous designer's signature on it, was being wrapped lavishly in shiny gilt paper printed with scarlet robins. 'Will Marco like it?' asked Polly anxiously, as she stuck a large red ribbon bow to the finished parcel.

'He'll love it,' Joanna assured her.

By noon of Christmas Eve Joanna's state of tension was only slightly less than Polly's. The tree was ablaze with lights, the table in the dining room festive with scarlet napkins and glittering Christmas crackers, a holly arrangement in the centre of the snowy white cloth. Wonderful smells filled the air in the kitchen, where a fillet of beef was nearing

perfection in the oven, surrounded by roasting potatoes. A pan of fragrant tomato and basil soup
sat on the stove, ready to decant into dishes for the
first course, and in the refrigerator Polly's favourite
lemon soufflé waited to round off a menu Joanna
had chosen with care to appeal to a palate used to
the sophisticated offerings of London restaurants.

When Marc arrived, at twelve-fifteen to the
minute, as promised, Joanna hung back while he
fended off the dog as he scooped up an excited
Polly, swinging her round a couple of times as he
always did. He set her on her feet then came towards Joanna, his smile guarded.

'Hello, Joanna.'

'Hello, Marc.' She took his proffered hand
briefly, then led the way into the house. 'Is it too
soon to say Merry Christmas?'

'Of course not. Merry Christmas to you both.'
He stood in the centre of the hall, smiling, looking
so attractive to Joanna that she felt shy.

Which was ridiculous, she told herself, all things
considered. Polly danced round him in a fever of
excitement, encapsulating all the news of the past
few weeks into one incoherent monologue which
ended only when he hugged the breath out of her,
then swung her up in his arms under the mistletoe
hanging from the hall light and kissed her on each
scarlet cheek.

Polly slid to the ground, pushing Joanna
forward. 'Now Jo, Marco.'

For a moment Joanna was sorely tempted to turn
tail and run, but the mockery in Marc's gleaming
black eyes put her on her mettle. She moved under
the mistletoe and held up her cheek, closing eyes

which flew open again in astonishment when Marc took her in his arms and kissed her hard on the mouth.'

'Merry Christmas once more,' he said softly, releasing her.

'I—I must see to the lunch,' said Joanna, backing away, her cheeks rivalling Polly's.

'Let's take Sunny for a run in the garden, Polly. You can help me get some things out of the car,' said Marc, a look of victory about him which sent Joanna off to the kitchen, routed.

The meal was a great success. Joanna's initial awkwardness soon wore off in the face of Marc's obvious effort to make the occasion a happy one for Polly. He was complimentary about the food, and the wine Joanna had chosen, wore his paper pirate's hat with panache and looked so much at home at the head of the table that Joanna began to wonder what on earth had possessed her to refuse his proposal. If she hadn't been so stubborn, her present problem would be no problem at all.

'That's a very pensive look,' said Marc quietly, when Polly was in the kitchen giving Sunny left-overs from the meal.

'Was it?' Joanna smiled brightly. 'I didn't mean to put a damper on things.'

'You couldn't.' Marc smiled, making her heart turn over. 'I wanted you to know I'm grateful for the way you've made Polly so happy, Joanna. I was worried about Christmas—afraid it might revive memories she'd find painful.'

'There've been one or two bad patches,' she admitted in an undertone. 'She asked me if her mother would have Christmas in heaven.'

'Bloody hell!'

'Quite. I said it was definite, because it's the birthday of Jesus.' Joanna smiled ruefully. 'I had to think on my feet, believe me.'

'You do very well,' he said gruffly. 'In fact, you make a wonderful mother. I must be honest—I didn't think so at first, but Rosa knew exactly what she was doing by handing Polly over to you.'

Joanna gazed into his intent eyes, taking her courage in both hands. 'Marc——' She broke off at the sight of Polly advancing slowly into the room, bearing the large crystal bowl of soufflé, with Sunny in hazardous attention. 'Goodness, darling, that must be heavy for you. Thank you very much.'

Joanna's sudden urge to confess was lost as Marc took the bowl from Polly and shooed Sunny from the forbidden territory of the dining-room. It was the wrong time, anyway, Joanna assured herself, as she served the pudding.

'None for you?' Marc tasted his with pleasure. 'Not dieting, are you?' His eyes rested on the fuller curves outlined by her crimson sweater. 'I fancy you've put on a little weight since I saw you last, but it suits you.'

Joanna's stomach gave a sickening lurch as Polly, to her infinite relief, interrupted with a plea for a present-giving session later when lunch was over. 'Marco won't be here tomorrow,' she entreated, her face rivalling the Christmas tree once permission was given.

'But only once we've helped Joanna clear every-thing away,' warned Marc as they rose from the table.

Once the kitchen was in order, Joanna sent the other two out for a quick session in the garden with Sunny and a ball while she went upstairs and made repairs to a face which felt shiny and hot after the rigours of the morning. In her full-length mirror she scrutinised herself in profile anxiously, but decided that other than a slight new fullness of curve here and there her secret was safe. For the time being.

'Jo!' called Polly from downstairs. 'Come *on*.'

When Joanna joined the others in the drawing-room she felt a sharp pang of yearning. The elegantly shabby room, lit only by the logs crackling in the hearth and the lights on the tree, was a wonderfully welcoming place. The scene before her was the epitome of everything she held dear, not least because Marc held centre stage as he leaned an elbow on the chimney-piece, his chiselled features softened with amusement over the antics of Polly and her dog on the hearthrug.

He looked up, smiling. 'Polly's going to do the honours, Joanna. We've decided that you shall recline gracefully while Polly dishes out the presents.'

Joanna obediently settled herself on the worn brocade of the sofa, while Polly, beaming from ear to ear, presented her uncle with her offering, hanging over him anxiously as he exclaimed with unfeigned pleasure over the scarf.

Polly danced to the tree to get another parcel. 'Look, Marco, this is for you from Jo.'

Joanna's gift, which had taken some time to create, was a framed water-colour of Polly's head and shoulders. Marc gazed at it for so long in silence

that Joanna wanted to fidget as Polly was doing,
while they waited for his verdict.

'Do you like it, Marco?' Polly demanded at last.
'Isn't Jo clever? I sat *very* still. *And* I kept it a
secret! Look, there's my dimple——'

'It's exquisite, *cara*. I'm overwhelmed.' Marc
walked over to Joanna and raised her hand to his
lips, an oddly bleak look in his eyes. 'My grateful
thanks. You're very talented.' He turned to Polly,
smiling again. 'These are the best presents I've ever
had. I shall wear the scarf always, and hang the
drawing on the wall in my new flat. You shall
choose where, if you like, Polly. Now the painters
are finished you can come to stay with me during
the holidays.'

But Polly was more interested in the presents
Marc produced from behind the tree. She crowed
with delight over a small pair of Levis and some
track shoes, too taken up with trying them on to
notice Marc's departure from the room until he
came back with a small bicycle, complete with bal-
ancing wheels. She fairly screeched with excitement, throwing herself at her tall uncle like a
missile as she kissed him all over his face.

'You guessed!' she said, almost tearful with delight as she slid down to perch herself on the bicycle.
'Please come outside. I want to ride it.'

'Not so fast,' he said firmly, taking a small
package from his pocket. 'Don't you think Jo
should have her present first?'

Joanna felt nervous, remembering the porcelain
horse, but she smiled with genuine pleasure to find
Marc's gift was a relatively inexpensive but pretty
antique brooch in the shape of a swan.

'Oh, look!' said Polly happily. 'Just like in *The Ugly Duckling*!'

'It's quite lovely,' said Joanna fervently, and jumped to her feet to thank Marc, only to sit down again with an inelegant thump as the room swam round sickeningly for a moment.

'What's the matter?' demanded Marc sharply.

'Just dizzy,' gasped Joanna. 'I'll be fine in a minute. Must be the heat of the fire.'

'You'd better sit quietly for a bit while I take Polly out on her bike,' he ordered. 'Do you do this often?'

'No.' She smiled brightly. 'I'm fine, honestly. Do take Polly out for a ride. And thank you so much for the brooch.'

Joanna was glad of the breathing-space while the other two were outside, gloomily convinced Marc must think her a total hypochondriac. After a while she pinned the brooch to her sweater and got up to put the kettle on for tea that had lately become an addiction.

When the fading light sent Marc and Polly in at last the latter was sent up to wash while Marc carried a tea-tray into the drawing-room for Joanna.

'What time do you have to leave?' she asked.

'I'll wait until Polly's in bed. I'm not going far.' His smile was sardonic. 'You haven't asked where I'm spending Christmas, but just in case you need to get in contact for some emergency of Polly's, I'm indulging in one of those impersonal, every-thing-laid-on type of Christmas breaks in a Cotswold hotel.' He handed her a card. 'Here's the number.'

Polly's return ruled out further conversation. From then on until Polly's bathtime and subsequent settling down to sleep, there was no further exchange between them until Marc came downstairs after reading to Polly, his face so hostile that Joanna eyed him in trepidation.

'What's the matter?' she asked.

Marc's brows rose slightly over eyes as hard and cold as jet. 'Polly's just let me in on a very interesting little secret. Only she was guilt-stricken afterwards, because she wasn't supposed to tell.'

'Tell what?' said Joanna, her heart sinking.

'Apparently Jack and Charlie Lavenham heard their mummy telling their daddy,' he said with deadly mimicry, 'that you are expecting a baby.'

CHAPTER NINE

JOANNA whitened as she faced the sudden blaze of anger in Marc's eyes. 'I—I asked Mary not to tell George.' She hugged her arms across her chest. 'I had no idea Polly knew.'

'Nevertheless she does know. As do the Lavenhams. Possibly Swancote *en masse* as well. Everyone, in fact, except me.' Marc pounced, seizing her by the elbows. 'When, Joanna?'

'July,' she said hoarsely.

Marc released her, standing back, his face expressionless. 'Then it's mine, not Paul's. Unless there's someone else in the running, of course.'

His tone lashed Joanna into sudden fury. 'If you have any doubts on that score,' she spat, 'get out. Now.'

'Not on your sweet life. I want a few things cleared up.' Marc stood with long legs apart, his arms folded. 'If the date is July, I must be the father. Is that right?'

'Yes,' she said flatly.

'Quite a bombshell! I thought you couldn't have more children.'

Joanna's chin lifted proudly. 'So did I. But it seems my doctor was mistaken. Utterly ludicrous, isn't it? If Paul had been the kind of husband prepared to take me for better or worse as he was supposed to, he might have achieved his family in the end after all. Not that I could have guaranteed him a son, of course. The child I lost was a girl. So is Polly.'

'For the moment,' said Marc menacingly, advancing on her, 'and just for once, I'm not interested in Polly, and certainly not in Paul bloody Clifford. I'm interested in you, and me, and our baby. When were you going to tell me——?' He stopped dead, suddenly white as his shirt. 'Or were you planning to arrange things so you didn't have to?'

Joanna stared at him in horror. 'You think I'd have——?' She swallowed, gulped hard, then brushed him aside and tore from the room to the small cloakroom off the hall.

When she returned to the drawing-room, ashen-faced but relatively composed Marc was standing in front of the dying fire, his face so masklike that Joanna had no clue as to his feelings.

'Perhaps you'd go now,' she said distantly. 'But first, purely for the record, you may care to know that I was a coward. I lacked the courage to tell you because it sounded like such out-and-out blackmail. Think about it. I wouldn't marry you before for the sole reason that I couldn't give you a child of your own. I just couldn't bring myself to come to you, cap in hand, just because by some practical joke of fate it seems I can, after all.'

'Why the hell not? I had a right to know!' he said bitterly.

'You couldn't have failed to know soon.' She tried a casual smile. 'If my present rate of expansion continues I'm likely to be what is known as "great with child" far sooner than I'd like.'

They stared at each other in hostile silence for a long, tense interval then Marc picked up his coat. 'I need some time to think,' he said wearily. 'Under the circumstances I find it damned impossible to understand your opposition to marriage. I, unlike Paul Clifford, want *my* child to know exactly who its father is. *Capisce*? If you won't marry me that's too bad. But don't imagine for a minute you'll bring up a child of mine in ignorance of the fact that Marc Anstey is its father.' He glared at her. 'I suppose you hate the thought of having my baby.'

'Do you expect me to be thrilled to bits?' she demanded.

'No. I suppose not. On which note I'll bid you goodnight, Joanna. Thanks for lunch.' To her dismay he strode past her, grim-faced, then turned in the doorway. 'I forgot,' said Marc, in a tone which flayed. 'Merry Christmas.'

Afterwards Joanna had very little recollection of how she got through the following day at the Lavenhams'. Looking back on it, she knew that she'd opened gifts, drunk sherry and pulled crackers, eaten turkey and joined in all the merriment and festivities, gone for the ritual walk afterwards, and returned to play silly games and drink tea and hand round mince pies.

'Are you all right, Jo?' asked Mary in private when Joanna said goodbye.

Joanna hesitated, then shrugged wearily. 'You told George; the twins heard; they told Polly; she told Marc.' Joanna kissed Mary's guilt-flushed cheek. 'Don't worry, love. He had to know some time.'

Once Polly was in bed it was a strange experience to sit alone on the evening of Christmas Day. When her father was alive Joanna had brought friends home for Christmas, the more the merrier as far as Richard Swan was concerned. Then she'd married Paul and Christmas had become a commercial, glossy affair. But at least it was never quiet like this, she thought, feeling so lonely and depressed that at long last she gave up the struggle with her pride and rang Marc's expensive Cotswold hotel, surprised that instead of paging Mr Anstey the receptionist put her through to his room immediately.

'Joanna,' she said tentatively when he answered.

'Joanna?' His voice sharpened. 'What's the matter? Is it Polly? Or are you ill——?'

'No, no, nothing like that. I just wanted a word with you.'

There was a long, unbearable pause.

'So talk, then,' he said at last.

'I wondered,' she said coolly, 'if you'd have time to call back here before returning to London.'

'Why?'

'There appears to be something wrong with Polly's bike.'

'I see. Stupid of me. For a moment I hoped you wanted to discuss our little mutual problem.'

Joanna scowled. Marc was right. She did. There was nothing at all wrong with Polly's bicycle. 'We could,' she said colourlessly. 'If you wish.'

'Since when were you so magnanimous about *my* wishes?'

'I agree there are things to discuss——' she began stiffly.

'You bet your sweet life there are!' There was a pause. 'All right, Joanna. I'll come tomorrow afternoon. I'm committed to lunch with someone here first.'

'Thank you,' said Joanna formally.

'I can't stay long. I've got an appointment later in London.'

'I'm only too grateful you can fit a visit to Swan House into your busy schedule at all,' she said sweetly. 'Goodnight.'

'Wait,' said Marc peremptorily. 'Don't hang up. How was Polly's day?'

'On the whole very good. She cried a bit first thing, when we opened her Christmas stocking together in bed.

'Because she always did that with Rosa.' Marc's voice grew huskier. 'All day I've been thinking I should have been there too.'

In my bed? thought Joanna. 'It was your choice to stay away,' she pointed out. 'But don't worry, she was fine the rest of the day. The noise and commotion at the Rectory were just what she needed.'

'It was pretty lively here, too,' he said heavily. 'But it was no substitute for a family Christmas with Rosa and Polly.'

'No,' said Joanna, sighing. 'I don't suppose it was.'

'I'll see you tomorrow, then.'

'Thank you for sparing the time. Goodnight.' Joanna put the phone down very carefully, then, unable to face televised Christmas jollity alone, she went out for a brief, chilly stroll in the garden with Sunny before retiring to bed with the latest bestseller, her gift from Mary.

The morning of Boxing Day passed very
pleasantly. Several neighbours called in from time
to time for a drink and a chat, kind in their efforts
to cheer Joanna up in her first Christmas alone at
Swan House, and later, glad to repay Mary's hos-
pitality for the day before, Joanna invited Jack and
Charlie to lunch. After a boisterous, noisy meal in
the kitchen, she played a fast and furious game of
Snap on the drawing-room carpet with the children,
took them for a short walk afterwards with the dog,
then suggested they draw for a while on the kitchen
table. When George Lavenham arrived to collect
his sons he was astonished to find peace and quiet
reigning at Swan House, as the three children vied
with each other to create the best likeness of Sunny.

Agreeing to his sons' demands of a few extra
minutes to finish their masterpieces, George admired the artists' work, then accepted Joanna's
offer of a glass of sherry in the drawing-room.

'I'm rather glad of a chance for a quiet chat, Jo,'
said George, leaning an arm on the chimney piece,
just as Marc had done.

Joanna eyed him, resigned, thinking how
handsome he looked with his windblown fair hair
above the heavy white sweater knitted by his
mother, the silk scarf Mary had given him knotted
at his open collar. George Lavenham in mufti
looked more like a movie actor than a man of the
cloth.

'About the baby, you mean.'

George nodded. 'I just wanted you to know that
if you don't want to marry the chap, it won't make
any difference to Mary and me. We'll give you any
help and support you want, Jo.'

Joanna, fully expecting a homily on why she should persuade Marc to do the decent thing, burst into tears.

George put down his glass hurriedly and pulled her up into his arms. He held her close, smoothing her hair, undismayed by the torrent of scalding tears soaking his new sweater. 'There, there,' he said soothingly. 'You've had a rotten time of it lately.'

These kind words, far from drying Joanna's tears, made her cry all the harder, and George fished in his pocket for the large clean handkerchief Mary always provided for use in emotive situations among his parishioners. He scrubbed at her face energetically, winning a wobbly smile as reward. He smiled back encouragingly, then hugged Joanna hard, giving her a smacking kiss, whereupon an ungentle hand hauled him off and hit the Reverend Mr Lavenham square on the jaw with a blow which felled him to the floor.

Joanna dropped to her knees beside George, blazingly angry as she turned to glare up at Marc Anstey, who bent to haul her back up again while George leapt lightly to his feet, his face alight with amusement.

'What in heaven's name do you think you're doing?' demanded Joanna in a rage.

'Dr Morley, I presume,' snarled Marc, advancing on George, who made things rather worse by trying hard not to laugh.

'Don't be stupid, Marc!' said Joanna, incensed. 'This is George Lavenham.'

'Hell—you're not the vicar?' asked Marc in dismay.

George grinned, fingering his jaw. 'That's me. But if you think I'm going to turn the other cheek you're mistaken!'

Colour surged in Marc's dark, arrested face. He spread both hands in apology, stifling a curse. 'Lord, I don't know what to say. Seeing the lights in the kitchen, I came in that way, and Polly sent me straight in here. I thought Joanna was resting. When I found you together I just saw red.' He eyed George ruefully. 'I've had a few scuffles in my time, but I've never hit a clergyman before.'

'You only managed it this time because you took George by surprise,' observed Joanna nastily. 'He boxed for his college.'

'Comes in handy at the youth club,' said George cheerfully. 'Any time you fancy lending a hand we could use you. That's a punishing left.'

Marc smiled remorsefully. 'You're taking this very well.'

'George may be, but I'm not!' snapped Joanna. 'I don't see what business it is of yours who you find in my drawing-room.'

'It is when the man's kissing you!'

They confronted each other like gladiators, oblivious of George, who looked on with deep enjoyment as he finished his sherry.

'I happen to think that what I do, and who I do it with, is entirely my own affair,' said Joanna bitingly.

'Oh, do you! In my opinion the fact that you're expecting my baby makes it very much *my* affair,' returned Marc.

'Rubbish! Besides, George was kissing me purely by way of comfort. Being pregnant seems to have affected my tear ducts. I started crying when he assured me of combined Lavenham support whatever I decide to do.'

'You know bloody well what you're going to do. You're going to marry me, you maddening woman.' Marc turned to George in appeal. 'Surely you agree?'

'Have you asked her?' queried George casually.

'Of course I've asked her!' Marc raked a hand through his hair violently.

'No, you haven't!' contradicted Joanna.

Marc gave her a look which brought the blood to her cheeks. 'I don't want to embarrass Lavenham here, but if necessary I can recall the exact time and place of my proposal!'

She sniffed. 'You haven't asked me since you heard about the baby.'

There was silence for a moment or two.

'I thought,' said Marc with care, 'that you would realise, without my having to repeat it, that the proposal still stood. I've never withdrawn it. You were the one against marriage. Not me.'

Joanna's eyes blazed with scorn. 'How like a man! Can't you see that finding I was pregnant changed everything? Of course I needed to be asked again! Besides,' she added truculently, 'I thought you might have changed your mind. I don't want you tied to me against your will—I've had enough of that.'

'When will you get it through your head that I am nothing like Paul Clifford?' He ground his teeth impotently. 'The bastard wrecked your confidence and gave you such a jaundiced view of men in

general you can't trust anyone, most of all me, as
far as I can see.'

'But in a roundabout way,' put in George
peaceably, 'he was actually instrumental in bringing
you two together.'

Marc's eyes narrowed thoughtfully. 'You're right.
He was. For that, at least, I suppose I should be
grateful.'

'By which I gather you love Joanna.' George
smiled. 'It's all that matters, really, you know.'

Marc turned slowly to meet Joanna's startled
eyes. 'He's right, of course. It is all that matters.
I love you. These past few weeks have taught me
that as long as you let me play a part in your life—
preferably the lead,' he added with a wry grin, 'I'll
accept your terms.'

Joanna stared at him dumbly, wondering how to
find a way to let him know she preferred his original
idea.

'Um—look,' said George apologetically, 'tell me
to push off and mind my own business if you like,
but my experience as Mary's husband emboldens
me to suggest that Joanna may have changed her
mind. About marriage, I mean.'

'Is that right?' demanded Marc, seizing Joanna's
hands.

'Yes,' she said faintly.

'Louder, please.'

'Yes, yes, *yes*!'

Marc caught Joanna in his arms and kissed her
soundly, then shook her very gently. 'Why?'

She shrugged. 'Because I need a father for this
baby of ours, why else? And because I love you,'

she added casually, her smile suddenly radiant as he crushed her close, oblivious of George.

Suddenly the door burst open and in came three small people waving pieces of paper.

'Which one is the best, Marco?' Polly demanded. She turned to the twins in triumph. 'He's *my* uncle—he'll say mine is best!'

Six months later, on a hot afternoon in July, a familiar black BMW roared through the village of Swancote and took the turn into the drive of Swan House at reckless speed, spurting gravel in all directions. Marc Anstey took a flying leap from the car and burst into the house, taking the stairs two at a time to reach the bedroom. A nurse rose from beside the bed, startled, as the tall, dishevelled man gathered her patient into his arms and kissed her with a passion the nurse obviously felt out of place in a room where only a short time before the lady in question had been delivered of a child. Nurse Roberts was only slightly mollified when the harassed father turned to her urgently afterwards, demanding assurances on the health of his wife.

'This is my husband,' said Joanna unnecessarily.

'How do you do, Mr Anstey?' said the nurse, turning away to the cradle. 'You need have no fears about your wife. She did beautifully. Would you like to hold the baby?'

Marc received the small bundle into his arms with delight. He settled himself on the bed beside Joanna, one arm around her shoulders, the other holding the baby with an expertise which deeply impressed his wife.

'What a clever girl your mother is,' he said to the small, sleeping face.

'Not so clever,' said Joanna as the nurse left them alone together. 'I was up at dawn this morning, so determined to finish a chapter of the new book I ignored certain early warnings from young Anstey here. By the time I contacted Roger Morley he wouldn't let me risk the journey to Swanford General. He managed to get hold of Nurse Roberts, and we managed the whole thing here between us.'

'How about Polly?' asked Marc eventually, when he could bring himself to stop kissing Joanna by way of fervent appreciation.

'I got her off with Mary without letting on what was happening. Mary came straight back here after taking the children to school, needless to say.' Joanna grinned. 'She said someone had to keep boiling kettles, the way they do in films. Heaven knows what she did with all the hot water—made tea, probably. She's giving Polly supper with the twins before bringing her home, but promised to keep the secret. Polly will be thrilled to bits. She thought she had to wait another week before this little bundle arrived.'

'So did I!' Marc's arm tightened as he bent to kiss her again. 'I nearly went into orbit when Mary rang the office. It was a piece of hard news I wasn't prepared for, believe me.' He removed his arm from Joanna's shoulder to settle the baby more comfortably. 'By the way, how do I address this little personage? When I spoke to you last you were still dithering about a name.'

Joanna smiled at him smugly. 'I thought Richard. My father would be pleased.'

Marc stared at her blankly. 'But that's a boy's name.'

'Well done, Mr Hotshot Journalist! Of course it's a boy's name. We've got a son, darling.' Joanna began to laugh as Marc began unwrapping the little bundle to see for himself.

'So we have!' he said in wonder, then handed the baby to Joanna to put back together again, a process young Richard Anstey objected to in a way which brought the nurse running.

'Try him on the breast, Mrs Anstey,' she instructed, giving Marc a look intended to send him packing.

Marc Anstey, used to confronting far more difficult personalities than Nurse Roberts, settled himself firmly alongside Joanna on the bed again, shocking the poor woman to the core by helping his son find the source of nourishment he was yelling for, whereupon Nurse Roberts retired from the room, routed.

'You've upset her,' observed Joanna, gazing down at the small face at her breast.

'Too bad,' said Marc, unrepentant as he gazed at his wife and son. 'She may as well get used to having me around——' He frowned. 'How long is she staying?'

'Only for a day or two. She can sleep in the spare room.'

But Marc was no longer interested in the nurse. 'You know it's a funny thing, darling, I was completely convinced we'd have another daughter.'

Joanna smiled tenderly at his slip. 'Since we're already blessed with Polly I think a son is a nice idea. We can have another girl next time.'

Marc gazed at her in awe. 'What a woman! I thought new mothers always said "never again" at this particular juncture.'

'I can understand that, I suppose,' she conceded, thinking about it. 'It's dashed hard work, producing a baby——'

'Not for me, it isn't!'

They laughed together, disturbing their son. Joanna transferred him carefully to her other side, pulling a face. 'I'm a bit clumsy about all this, Marc. I hope I get better as I go along.'

'For me you're perfection as you are,' he said matter-of-factly, bringing a glow to her eyes as he bent to lean his cheek against her hair.

Later, when the nurse had wheeled the baby away, Marc smoothed the hair back from Joanna's forehead with a caressing hand. 'Are you tired, my angel?'

'A bit, but so happy.' She smiled. 'I think I'll have a little snooze before Polly comes.'

'While I shall take a bath and have a long, celebratory glass of something.' Marc stretched as he stood up, shaking his head. 'A son! Can you believe, darling, that I had no idea until now that I quite fancied one? Not that a daughter wouldn't have been just as welcome——'

'But having Polly had already taken care of that.' Joanna stretched, wincing a little. 'It's perfectly natural. We're lucky, we've got one of each—who knows? One day we might have two of each.'

He laughed. 'I applaud your enthusiasm!' He paused, looking down at her. 'I'm a lucky man. You were so right, Joanna. Giving Polly to you really was the perfect solution.'

She smiled. 'Not quite. What we have now is perfect in Polly's eyes; she's got her wish about a family just like the Lavenhams.'

'Ah, but she's one up on the twins now. She's got a baby brother as well—cousin really,' he added, chuckling.

Joanna shook her head. 'No fear. Polly's as much our child as the scrap who arrived today, Marc. Rosa gave her to us.'

'And gave you into my hands in the process,' he said, kissing her. 'Once I accidentally hit on the one sure way to get you to marry me, that is.'

'Clever devil!' Joanna smiled drowsily. 'Not, I hasten to add, that I'm sorry you did. After six months of connubial bliss, husband dear, I realise that marriage—for you and me, anyway—was the most perfect solution of all.'

Holiday Romance

Make your holiday extra special with four
new Romances from Mills & Boon.

PLANTATION SUMMER
Angela Devine

VENDETTA BRIDE
Rebecca King

TREACHEROUS PATH
Joanna Neil

A HEART DIVIDED
Lee Stafford

Four Romances by four
popular authors have been
specially chosen for this
exciting gift selection.

What could be easier to pack
for your holiday!

Published: 12th June 1992   Price: £6.80

Next Month's Romances

Each month you can choose from a world of variety in romance with Mills & Boon. Below are the new titles to look out for next month, why not ask either Mills & Boon Reader Service or your Newsagent to reserve you a copy of the titles you want to buy — just tick the titles you would like to order and either post to Reader Service or take it to any Newsagent and ask them to order your books.

Please save me the following titles: Please tick | √

DARK RANSOM	Sara Craven	
TAKEN BY STORM	Sandra Field	
LESSON TO LEARN	Penny Jordan	
WALK UPON THE WIND	Patricia Wilson	
WHIRLPOOL	Madeleine Ker	
COERCION TO LOVE	Michelle Reid	
LOVE RULES	Ann Charlton	
HIDDEN MEMORIES	Vanessa Grant	
MAID FOR MARRIAGE	Sue Peters *(Faraway Places)*	
THE SINGING TREE	Anne Weale	
LOVE IS A RISK	Jennifer Taylor	
MIRACLES CAN HAPPEN	Stephanie Howard *(Starsign)*	
BLOSSOMING LOVE	Deborah Davis	
STRONG MAGIC	Christine Greig	
THE STORY PRINCESS	Rebecca Winters	
GOBLIN COURT	Sophie Weston	

If you would like to order these books from Mills & Boon Reader Service please send £1.70 per title to: Mills & Boon Reader Service, P.O. Box 236, Croydon, Surrey, CR9 3RU and quote your Subscriber No:..(If applicable) and complete the name and address details below. Alternatively, these books are available from many local Newsagents including W.H.Smith, J.Menzies, Martins and other paperback stockists from 8th June 1992.

Name:...

Address:...

....Post Code:.......................

To Retailer: If you would like to stock M&B books please contact your regular book/magazine wholesaler for details.

You may be mailed with offers from other reputable companies as a result of this application.
If you would rather not take advantage of these opportunities please tick box ☐